BARBARA CARTLAND'S YEAR OF ROYAL DAYS

BARBARA CARTLAND'S

YEAR OF
ROYAL DAYS

Lennard Publishing 1988

Lennard Publishing
a division of Lennard Books Ltd

Lennard House
92 Hastings Street
Luton, Beds LU1 5BH

British Library in Publication Data
is available for this title.

ISBN 1 85291 031 3

First published 1988
© Barbara Cartland 1988

Phototypeset in Goudy
by Goodfellow & Egan, Cambridge

Cover design by Pocknell and Co.

Printed and bound in Great Britain by
Butler & Tanner Ltd, Frome and London

Contents

JANUARY

January 1st   1540

A Royal romeo is frustrated

King Henry VIII had chosen Anne of Cleves as his fourth wife from a portrait. The Marriage Treaty was drawn up.

Anne arrived in England just after Christmas 1539 and rested at Canterbury. Her meeting with Henry was to take place in five days.

At Greenwich the King became increasingly impatient. At last, too restless to wait any longer, he had an idea. Anne was to arrive at Rochester on New Year's Eve. He would surprise her there on New Year's Day, bursting in on her as in his youth he had burst in on Katharine and her maidens, disguised as Robin Hood.

When Anne recovered her composure they would laugh together, he would kiss her and give her sables for her neck and throat, and a furred cap.

On New Year's Eve the King and a few companions dressed themselves in capes of grey velvet and set off on their romantic errand. King Henry rode hard for the coast, eager to see his bride, eager, as he confided to Cromwell, "to nourish love".

When he arrived he walked into Anne's rooms unannounced and was, "marvellously astonished and abashed."

Anne was exceedingly plain!

Good manners forced him to embrace her – a chaste kiss of welcome.

His "discontentment and misliking of her person" could hardly be hidden. His Majesty left as suddenly as he had arrived.

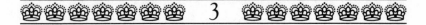

January 2nd   1762

Death of The Empress Elizabeth of Russia

The Empress Elizabeth died on this day. She had been, according
to the English Ambassador, backward in any sort of civilised
behaviour. At the Court only half her attendants could read and
only a third could write.

The Grand Duke Peter managed to alleviate his boredom by
boring holes in the floors of his apartment so that he could peep
into the Empress's private rooms and watch her making love.

January 3rd   1661

H.M. King Charles II waits for 'a shave'

"The first time", Samuel Pepys wrote, when he saw the *Beggar
Bush*, "That ever I saw women come upon the stage".

Owing to a lack of female players men still had to play women's
roles.

King Charles II arrived early at a performance and found the
actors were not ready to begin. Impatiently the King demanded to
know the cause of the delay.

"The Queen is not yet shaved, Sire!" His Majesty was told.

The King laughed and accepted the excuse which served to
divert him till the male Queen could be effeminated.

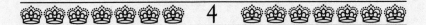

January 4th   48 B. C.

The Venus of the Nile

An itinerant vendor pleaded outside the Palace Gates that he might show his wares to Roman troops installed there.

In the carpet over his shoulder, half suffocated was the Queen of Egypt. Caesar was busy with State papers in the Royal apartments.

"A Gift for the mighty Caesar," the vendor said.

"I have no need of tawdry gifts," Caesar snapped.

"But the gift is unique!" the vendor replied and with a flash of his hand rolled out the carpet.

Caesar was fifty-three years old. Queen Cleopatra was twenty-one. She was not Egyptian but Macedonian – skin as white as milk, eyes as blue as the Aegean, hair of burnished gold.

Caesar looked, loved and was conquered.

January 5th   1757

Attempted assassination

Between five and six on this evening, H.M. King Louis XV of France was getting into his coach at Versailles to go to the Trianon. A man, who had lurked about the colonnades for two days, moved up to it.

He jostled the Dauphin, and stabbed the King under the right arm with a long knife. His Majesty was, however, wearing two thick coats, so the blade did not penetrate deeply.

At first the King thought the man had only pushed against him then putting his hand to his side he felt blood and realised he had been stabbed.

The injury was not serious but Robert Frances Damien was tortured and killed by being publicly torn to pieces by horses.

January 6th   1927

A tearful farewell

H.R.H. The Duke and Duchess of York set sail from Portsmouth on board the battle cruiser *Renown* for an intensive tour of Australia and New Zealand. They left their eight month old daughter, the future Queen Elizabeth II, in the charge of Queen Mary and the Strathmore grandparents.

"I felt very much leaving on Thursday," the Duchess wrote. "Baby was so sweet playing with the buttons on Bertie's uniform that it quite broke me up."

January 7th   1536

H.M. Queen Katharine of Aragon dies

Years of insults and deprivations had not broken the Queen's courage nor her serenity. She died with the same humble confidence which had marked her life.

Although it was rumoured at the time that she had been poisoned it was probably cancer.

When the news of her death at Kimbolton reached London King Henry VIII adorned himself from head to toe in exultant yellow and celebrated the event with a Mass, a Banquet, dancing and jousting.

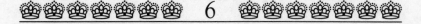

January 8th   1864

A Prince in a petticoat

There was a hockey match on the ice covering Virginia Water.
The Prince of Wales was playing and he arranged for a large
elaborate luncheon to be served beside the lake. Ice gleamed in the
sunshine and everybody was in the highest spirits.

Princess Alexandra arrived at eleven o'clock. She chatted with
all her friends, and ate a large luncheon. Several times during the
morning and afternoon she was watched being drawn swiftly around
the ice on a sledge.

Shortly after the Princess arrived back at Frogmore she
complained of feeling unwell and the local doctor was called.

He arrived just in time to deliver a baby boy – Prince Albert
Victor. It was so unexpected that no layette had been prepared and
the child was wrapped in one of Lady Macclesfield's petticoats.

January 9th   1683

The King's Evil

H.M. King Charles II in Council at Whitehall, today, issued
orders for the future regulation of the ceremony of Touching for the
King's Evil.

Specific control was exercised over those who attended the
public healings. The 'King's Evil', named Scrofula, consisted of
tumours on the victim's neck, but many people were keen to be
touched by the King.

The custom originated with King Edward the Confessor who miraculously cured a young woman of the disease by washing her neck with his own hands.

King Francis I of France and Queen Elizabeth are recorded to have healed the diseased by touch.

Queen Elizabeth was the first to give out coins called 'touch-pieces'.

Dr. Johnson gave the 'touch-piece' he received from Queen Anne to the British Museum. She was the last Sovereign to perform the ceremony.

January 10th   1936

Last words

When King George V was on his death-bed his Doctor while knowing it would be impossible, said to cheer him up:

"You are getting better, Sir. You will soon be able to go to Bognor for a holiday."

"Bugger Bognor," the King replied.

They were the Monarch's last words.

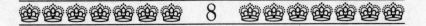

January 11th   1781

H.R.H. Prince William's ill-fated love

Prince William son of King George III fell in love with the oustandingly pretty Julia Fortescue. They met at a Ball at St. James's, danced together all the evening and wooed over the following weeks in a series of inadequately secret assignations in Green Park.

The Prince wanted to marry Julia – he had wanted to marry a surprising number of the girls he had met. Unfortunately the affair had not the remotest chance of reaching a happy conclusion.

Miss Fortescue was packed off to Scotland. The Prince had to return to the Navy and exiled to distant parts of the world.

January 12th   1871

Love and marriage

Prince Si Ahmed a young Arab ruler from Southern Algeria was visiting Bordeaux. A romantic figure, he saw as he moved with his entourage of guards, black slaves and courtiers, a beautiful girl feeding a number of carrier pigeons.

Aurélie Piccard, a little provincial, was apprenticed to a milliner.

The Prince tried to buy her but was told that she was not for sale, but she could be married.

Impetuous because he had lost his heart the Prince and Aurélie, after some difficulties with the Church, were married in January 1871.

Despite gloomy forebodings they were extremely happy and when Si Ahmed became an even more mighty Shareif he never took another wife, while Aurélie became an invincible power in the Sahara and all over Algeria.

She held not only the Sheikh but his tribe captive by her love.

January 13th   1923

Third time lucky

Twice in two years had H.R.H. Prince Albert Duke of York proposed to Lady Elizabeth Bowes Lyon.

King George V said to his son:

"You will be a lucky man if she accepts you."

When Prince Albert proposed for the third time Lady Elizabeth accepted. In triumph the Prince telegraphed his mother, Queen Mary, who was at Sandringham House in Norfolk:

'All right – Bertie'.

January 14th   1809

Duke or darling?

H.R.H. Frederick, Duke of York, had set up house with his Mistress, Mrs Clarke. She was good-looking, but her real charms were intellectual for she was daring, amusing and brilliant. The Duke of York was completely infatuated.

After a few years, however, the passion burned itself out, but in January 1809 a scandal developed due to accusations that Mrs Clarke had taken money to influence promotions in the Army.

It could not be proved that the Duke knew about the money or was just influenced by Mrs Clarke in the promotions he had made. Nevertheless, the Duke resigned as Commander-in-Chief, as he had been made to look ridiculous. His love-letters to Mrs Clarke had been laughed at by the entire House of Commons and published in the National Press.

Mrs Clarke's drunken butlers as well as abandoned friends came forward to say how they heard the Duke and Mrs Clarke say 'Darling this' and 'Darling that'.

Children in the streets tossed up pennies and cried out 'Duke or Darling?' instead of 'Heads or Tails?'.

Two years later when the disreputable exposure had died down, the Duke of York was reinstated as Commander-in-Chief.

January 15th   1975

H.M. Queen Susan

H. H. King Leka I of Albania, son of the flamboyant King Zog, left his country in the arms of his mother three days after he was born.

He lived with his family in England during the War and then in Alexandria at the invitation of King Farouk of Egypt before moving to Madrid.

He was proclaimed King in 1961 in Paris in the presence of a hastily convened temporary National Assembly.

Fourteen years later, King Leka fell in love with Susan Cullen-Ward, a very attractive, fair-haired Australian girl, the daughter of a sheep farmer. They were married in Biarritz amid scenes of loyalty from Albanian monarchists.

Susan became the first Australian Queen, and she is very happy with her tall, intelligent husband. His dream is to return home and rule over the small mountainous country he has never seen.

January 16th   1901

The donkey cart is not required

H.M. Queen Victoria was unable to take her afternoon drive in her donkey cart in the Osborne grounds.

The doctors had said she must not do any more business and the despatch boxes are beginning to pile up.

On January twenty-first, the Prince of Wales, Prince George and the Kaiser arrived at Osborne but by the next day there was no hope.

The Queen was cradled in the arms of her grandson, the Kaiser, all her family stood around the bed. She looked at them and called them by their names. At half past six she died.

Soon after, May, the new Princess of Wales, wrote to her Aunt Augusta:

"Now she lies in her coffin in the Dining Room which is beautifully arranged as a Chapel. The coffin is covered with the Coronation robes and her little diamond Crown and the garter lie on a cushion above her head . . . . . . You would howl if you could see it all. . . . . ."

January 17th   1711

A woman's quarrel

The famous Duke of Marlborough, a great soldier, returned home in deep distress. H.M. Queen Anne had commanded him to bring her his wife Sarah's Seal of Order – the gold key – within three days.

The reason was that The Queen had quarrelled with the hot-blooded Duchess who she alleged had told her to "hold her tongue".

That the Duchess was out of office and favour delighted those who were spiteful and envious. At the end of the year Marlborough was dismissed and threatened with impeachment.

He and his wife left for the Continent to await the Queen's death. She died on 1st April 1714.

The Duke returned to a hero's welcome, crowds scattered flowers in front of his glass coach.

King George I who had succeeded, remarked in German, the only language he knew:

"My dear Duke, I hope your troubles are now all over."

January 18th   1833

'Little Boar' arrives in London

H.M. King William IV's meeting with Red Indians was cancelled. Members of a tribe of Red Indians from Michigan arrived in London to negotiate the sale of certain lands.

The Chief known as 'Little Boar' and his party were due to be presented on this day to the King. Unexpectedly the Chief's Squaw, 'Diving Moose' who was only twenty-six years old, suddenly died.

She was given a splendid funeral at which the Chief declared:

"I am not, I never was, a man of tears: but her loss made me shed many."

January 19th   1544

The Puckish Puritan

Like H.M. King Charles I before him, Oliver Cromwell hunted the Hampton Court deer.

He also delighted in the company of his old war time cronies. After a hard day at the Chase it was his custom to entertain at a private supper.

Once the table was cleared he would feel free to show a very English side of his personality – a schoolboyish boisterousness.

He would drink freely and encourage his friends to take part in pranks such as 'throwing cushions and putting live coals into their pockets and boots'.

Sometimes he would order a drum to be beaten and demand that his Foot Guards, like a pack of hounds, snatch meat from his table and tear it to pieces.

January 20th   1794

The first-born

Dowty Jordan Miller, actress and mistress of the Duke of
Clarence on January 20th at her home in Somerset Street,
presented him with a son. He was christened George and Sophia
followed in 1795.

The illegitimate family eventually consisted of five boys and five
girls.

The Duke, later King William IV, was a kind, if over-indulgent,
father. George was his favourite.

Ten children in thirteen years could be taxing for any mother but
Mrs. Jordan managed to sustain her energetic theatrical career.
After a week or two she was back on the stage wearing the breeches
which were so much a part of her success.

Lady Bessborough seeing her perform in September 1807, a few
weeks after the arrival of her tenth child, wrote:

"Mrs. Jordan was received with boundless applause: she is terribly
large, but her voice and acting still delightful."

January 21st   1793

Court mourning in Russia

The Empress Catherine the Great had watched the Revolution
in France with horror. French was the language of the Court in
Russia, French fashions and French men and women were
everywhere in St. Petersburg.

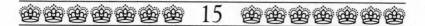

She was personally terrified of being assassinated and on the day the King and Queen of France went to the guillotine she imposed six weeks of Court mourning.

At 61 the Empress had lost all her teeth, was enormously fat and her legs were so swollen she could not walk. But her sexual appetite was as strong as ever and she had a new lover who was 22 years old.

January 22nd   1902

The end of John Brown

After the death of his mother, Queen Victoria, King Edward VII quickly removed or destroyed all the statues and busts of John Brown, the Highland servant she loved but who was detested by her family.

January 23rd   1743

The world's first Royal lift

H.M. Louis XV of France, an insatiable lover, was so anxious to lose no time between his apartment in the Palace of Versailles and that of his Mistress on the floor above, that in 1743 he installed the world's first lift.

The lift which was called 'The Flying Chair' was fixed on to the outside of the Palace and was operated from a private courtyard.

Few women could satisfy him. His wife Queen Maria bore him ten children and complained:

"I am either in bed, pregnant or brought to bed."

January 24th   1712

Military greatness

Frederick the Great of Prussia, son of Frederick William I and Sophia Dorothea, Princess of Prussia and Hanover, was born on this day.

In his childhood he was treated with extreme severity by his father, who disapproved of his studying anything other than military exercises.

The Queen arranged that he should flee to England and seek refuge with his maternal uncle, George II.

Before the escape could be effected the King found out and imprisoned his son. The Princess who implored the King to pardon her brother was thrown from one of the Palace windows.

Yet this Prince, having ascended to the throne, established the military renown of Prussia and became one of the most famous Generals in history.

January 25th   1308

Wedding of H.M. Edward II of England

The ceremony took place with great pomp in the Church of Notre Dame in Boulogne. But a shock awaited the thirteen year old bride, Isobella the Fair, on their arrival in England.

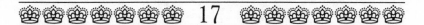

Her husband warmly embraced Piers Gaveston his favourite and gave him all the finest of her jewels and their joint wedding presents.

At the Coronation King Edward chose to sit on the bench with Piers rather than share his wife's 'couch'.

Influential Nobles tried to get rid of Gaveston but he evaded them until finally he was trapped at Scarborough in 1312 and beheaded.

On hearing of his death King Edward exclaimed:

"By God's soul, he acted as a fool. If he had taken my advice he would never have fallen into the hands of the Earls."

January 26th   1653

A Tomb of Love

After his wife Mumtaz Mahal died at 19, Shah Jehan Emperor of India was heart broken.

For the next twenty-two years Shah Jehan had 20,000 men working on her tomb. Its brick scaffolding cost £9 million and the building itself more that £18 million before it was finished in 1653.

The tomb was called the Taj Mahal which was a play on her name. It was and still is one of the wonders of the world.

No woman has ever had a more exquisite memorial erected to commemorate a great and enduring love.

January 27th   1956

Salute for the Queen

Queen Elizabeth and the Duke of Edinburgh embarked on a three-week tour of Nigeria. Before their arrival a rumour spread throughout Lagos that hats must be removed in front of the Queen.

Thousands of loyal subjects bought hats so that they could take them off when the Queen arrived.

January 28th   814

Charlemagne's Throne

King of the Franks and ruler of the Holy Roman Empire, King Charlemagne on his death was embalmed. He was dressed in the Royal robes with the crown on his head, and the sceptre in his hand.

Propped up on his Throne, he remained there for four hundred years until 1215. Then the Emperor Frederick II had the corpse removed and buried in a gold and silver casket in the Cathedral at Aix-la-Chapelle.

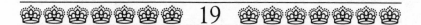

January 29th   1853

Royal football

The Empress Eugenie of France loved games and her favourite was 'potting the candles'.

After dinner footmen would place heaps of rubber balls on the salon floor. It was the task of the guests to kick them at the many lighted candles until all were extinguished.

The Empress excelled at this version of association football.

January 30th   1649

H.M. King Charles I beheaded

H.M. King Charles I, after being callously kept waiting for more than three hours in Whitehall Palace, was beheaded on a scaffold erected outside the Banqueting House.

The final request that the King made to his gaolers was that he should have a farewell interview with his children, Elizabeth and Henry. In an epistle to his son and heir he wrote:

"At worst, I trust I shall go before you to a better Kingdom, which God hath prepared for me, and me for it, through my Saviour Jesus Christ, to whose mercy I commend you, and all mine. Farewell, till we meet, if not on earth, yet in Heaven."

January 31st   1952

A last Royal farewell

H.M. King George VI went to London Airport to wave goodbye to Princess Elizabeth and the Duke of Edinburgh. They were flying to Kenya on the first stage of their tour to Australia and New Zealand.

Weak though he was, the King stood hatless in the icy cold with Queen Elizabeth, Princess Margaret and the Duke of Gloucester to see his daughter for the last time.

His Majesty died on February 6th.

In Nairobi Princess Elizabeth was watching wild life in the African bush, unaware that she was now The Queen.

FEBRUARY

February 1st   1908

Royal assassination

H.M. King Carlos of Portugal and his heir Prince Luis Filipe were assassinated as they rode in an open carriage in Lisbon.

It is not known whether the killers were isolated fanatics or agents of a hidden organisation such as the Carbonaria, a Republican Secret Society.

The young Prince Manoel who was riding with them was wounded and became the next King.

February 2nd   1839

Scandal at the Palace

Lady Flora Hastings, lady-in-waiting to Queen Victoria's mother, the Duchess of Kent, was not a popular figure at Court due to her rather severe and unforthcoming manner.

It did not help that she was on friendly terms with Sir John Conroy; the Queen intensely disliked and mistrusted her.

When she complained of pain and swelling of the stomach, the Queen had no doubt what the matter with the 'detestable person' was and wrote:

"Lady Flora had not been more that two days in the house before Lehzen and I discovered how exceedingly suspicious her figure looked – more we have since observed this and we have no doubt that she is – with child!! . . . . the horrid cause of all this is the Monster and Demon Incarnate whose name I forbear to mention but which is the first word of the second line of this page."

Lady Flora was persuaded to undergo a medical examination and was pronounced a virgin but the Queen remained sceptical. By June 27th the Queen was advised that she should leave at once.

Lady Flora died on July 5th, and a post-mortem revealed that the swelling of her stomach had been due to a growth on her liver.

February 3rd   1965

A young Prince Down Under

H.R.H. Prince Charles arrived at Timbertop, Australia and spent seven months getting to know the people, the country and himself.

His future equerry Squadron Leader David Checketts, said:

"I went out there with a boy and returned with a man."

Prince Charles later wrote of his experiences in the Gordonstoun Record:

"The first week I was there I was made to go out and chop up logs on a hillside in boiling hot weather. I could hardly see my hands for blisters."

The Prince also participated in weekend expeditions into the bush.

"You can't see anything but gum-tree upon gum-tree, which trends to become rather monotonous."

"You virtually have to inspect every inch of the ground you hope to put your tent on in case there are any ants or other ghastly creatures. There is one species of ant called Bull Ants which are three-quarters of an inch long, and they bite like mad!"

February 4th   1863

"Faits vos jeux"

On this day the fortunate subjects of H.M. King Charles III of Monaco were exempted from all rates and taxes.

This was due to the enormous revenue from the sole concession for running gaming in the Principality which the King had given to Monsieur Blanc.

As the visitors began to pour in, the new town was named after King Charles himself and called Monte Carlo.

February 5th   1952

Keepers' Day at Sandringham

A bright day of sunshine and frost as H.M. King George VI took part in a home shoot with his Keepers. He was in excellent form, shot well and planned the next day's sport.

After dinner he worked on some State papers. At midnight the policeman on duty in the garden saw His Majesty fixing the latch of his bedroom window.

Next morning when his Valet called the King with his tea, he found him lying peacefully but dead.

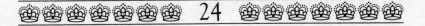

February 6th   1643

A Queen under fire

H.M. King Charles I's, Queen Henrietta Maria, arrived home from taking her eldest daughter, Mary, to join her future husband, William of Orange, in Holland.

The Queen disembarked at Bridlington, on the Yorkshire coast, a small village with a busy port. During the night, she had her first experience of being under fire in the Civil War.

As she slept, in a thatched cottage near the sea, four vessels under Parliamentarian Commanders sailed into the bay. They opened fire on the Royal ships and began a bombardment of the shore.

The Queen was hastily awakened and told she must seek safety in the ditches behind the village.

There was confusion and panic! One of the Maids of Honour went 'stark mad' and as the party of ladies ran towards the ditches, the Sergeant escorting them was shot, only twenty paces from Queen Henrietta Maria.

Her Majesty lay for two hours in a hole, with cannon-balls hurtling overhead.

February 7th   1977

"Rise Sir Norman"

The first couturier ever to be honoured by the K. C. V. O., Norman Hartnell designed the gowns in which Her Majesty Queen Elizabeth II was married and crowned.

His spectacular, glittering embroidery was enchanting and it was said: "He made every woman he dressed look like a fairy princess."

One seamstress alone did 3,000 hours of embroidery on the Coronation gown.

February 8th   1587

H.M. Mary Queen of Scots executed

At Fotheringay Castle the Queen's eyes were bound with a white cloth embroidered in gold which she herself had chosen for the purpose the night before.

She knelt down on the cushion in front of the block and cried: "Into your hands O Lord I commend my spirit."

The executioner did a poor job and it took three blows to sever her head. Afterwards he held it up and several times cried: "God Save the Queen" but the auburn locks came away from the skull and the head itself fell to the ground.

It was seen that Mary Stuart's own hair had turned grey, and was very short, so for her execution she had chosen to wear a wig.

Her favourite dog, a Skye terrier, was found hidden in her petticoats, and nothing would coax him away from her body.

February 9th   1921

A panther lives to tell the tale

H.R.H. The Prince of Wales visited India in 1921 and the Maharajas gave his party every possible animal to shoot taking the greatest care that His Royal Highness shot the best.

Staying with the Maharaja of Patiala the party had excellent sport, but late in the evening Lord Louis Mountbatten discovered that two panthers which they had killed had been taken from the Zoo, doped and laid out under suitable bushes.

A rare and valuable black panther had also been chosen. However when it was learnt that the Prince of Wales was not shooting on this day, they returned it to the Zoo and revived it.

February 10th   1840

A happy Royal marriage

Today Queen Victoria married Prince Albert of Saxe-Coburg-Gothe at the Chapel Royal, St James's. Before the wedding the Queen sent a note to her bridegroom:

"How are you today, and have you slept well? I have rested very well, and feel very comfortable today. What weather! I believe, however, the rain will cease."

"Send one word when you, my most dearly beloved bridegroom will be ready. Thy ever-faithful Victoria R."

At 12.30 the Queen set off from the Palace in a carriage with her mother and the Mistress of the Robes, to the Chapel Royal. Her wedding dress was of white satin, 'with a very deep flounce of Honiton lace.' She wore a diamond necklace and the sapphire brooch that Prince Albert had given her, with a wreath of orange blossoms.

February 11th   1765

A Royal joke

A petition was presented to H.M. King George III, by the Master peruke-makers of London.

They stated that the distress caused to themselves from the universal decline in their trade was due to gentlemen generally beginning to wear their own hair. The distressed peruke-makers prayed His Majesty for means of relief. The King with great self-control managed to return a gracious answer.

This incident, however, evoked innumerable jokes. Another petition was published from the *Body Carpenters*, urging the King to wear a wooden leg!

HENRICVS VIII REX
ANGLIE

January 1st 1540

H.M. King Henry VIII expected his fourth wife, Anne of Cleves to be a beauty. When he surprised her with a sudden meeting in Rochester on New Year's Day, her plainness left him 'marvellously astonished and abashed!

January 7th 1536

H.M. Queen Katharine of Aragon dies. The years had not broken the Queen's courage nor her serenity.

January 8th 1864

H.R.H. The Prince of Wales enjoyed a hockey match on ice covering Virginia Water. Princess Alexandra his wife arrived to watch at eleven o'clock. Later in the day she was delivered of a baby boy, and The Prince of Wales had a son – Prince Albert Victor.

January 13th 1923

H.R.H. Prince Albert, Duke of York, had twice proposed to Lady Elizabeth Bowes-Lyon. When she accepted his third proposal, he telegraphed his mother, Queen Mary: 'All right – Bertie'.

January 17th 1711

A Woman's Quarrel. H.M. Queen Anne quarrelled with the hot-blooded Duchess of Marlborough.

February 8th 1587

At Fotheringay Castle Mary Queen of Scots was blindfold with a white cloth embroidered in gold. She knelt before the block and cried 'Into your hands O Lord I commend my spirit'. It required three blows to sever her head.

February 10th 1840

Queen Victoria married Prince Albert of Saxe-Coburg-Gothe at the Chapel Royal, St James's. The queen wrote to Prince Albert, 'send one word when you, my most dearly beloved Bridegroom will be ready. Thy ever-faithful Victoria R'.

March 5th 1902

H.M. Edward VII enjoyed the secret of Marlborough House's Library. A hidden door was concealed by fake books. They had typically humorous titles: *Warm Receptions – by Burns; Lamb on the death of Wolfe*, and so on.

February 12th   1533

The Court astonished

A very odd little episode took place at the Court of King Henry
VIII, and was promptly reported to Eustace Chapuys, the Holy
Roman Emperor's Ambassador who made it his business always to
be well informed of current gossip.

Queen Anne Boleyn had emerged from her private apartment
into the hall, where a large crowd was assembled.

Seeing a particular friend among the company, 'one she loves
well' – she called out to him in sudden excitement, apparently à
propos of nothing, that – 'for the last three days I have had such an
incredible fierce desire to eat apples as I have never felt before.'

Then she added:

"The King says that it is a sign that I am with child, but I have
said No, it is not so at all."

As she finished she burst out laughing and disappeared back into
her rooms, while the onlookers stared at each other 'abashed and
uneasy'.

The Court fell happily on this juicy titbit of scandal. Anne was,
in fact, nearly three months pregnant by the time she made her
somewhat unconventional announcement.

February 13th   1374

The King of Sodom is crowned

H.M. King Henry III of France was crowned on this day, and
married a day later. When the crown was placed on his head he

complained that it hurt him, which was considered a bad omen.

Henry III was one of France's most controversial sovereigns. His morals caused much public disapproval and because he occasionally appeared at official ceremonies dressed as a woman he was nicknamed 'the King of Sodom.'

He had however several affairs with women and he was an excellent husband to Louise de Vaudemont. But his pampered physical appearance, his earrings and his entourage of attractive men called 'mignons' have left a dark cloud over his memory.

February 14th   1613

Giggles and snores on a Royal wedding day

H.R.H. Princess Elizabeth, daughter of H.M. James I, married Frederick Henry, Count of the Palatinate today in the Chapel Royal at Whitehall.

Unfortunately during the ceremony the Bride was overcome with bursts of laughter – it may have been due to nervous strain – but all the efforts of her former governess, Lady Hartington, were unable to check them.

In the evening the guests were entertained with a Masque. In spite of Inigo Jones's wonderful stage effects King James fell fast asleep during the performance.

February 15th   890

The clocks of H.M. King Alfred

Before the invention of clocks Alfred the Great ordered six tapers to be made for his daily use. As each taper was designed to burn for four hours he therefore had a means of knowing the time throughout the day.

Yet the wind blowing through the windows and doors, and chinks in the walls of the Chapel, made the tapers unreliable.

King Alfred, therefore, designed a lantern from animal horn in which he enclosed the tapers.

This proved to be far more reliable and was the world's first clock.

February 16th   1908

Prizes and fashions for Royal dogs

At the 53rd Dog Exhibition at the Crystal Palace, H.M. Queen Alexandra won four First Prizes with her Basset Hounds.

Luxury dogs had their own fashions. King Edward VII's mistress, Lillie Langtry, had her poodles clipped to read L. L.

In Paris a 'Dog Chauffeur' was equipped with goggles to follow his mistress into her automobile.

The Grand Duke Michael of Russia ordered for his fox-terrier a collar with coral and another with turquoises.

The wife of a Khedive gave her dog a lace jabot and overcoat with broad revers of green velvet.

February 17th   1986

A missile hits H.M. The Queen

H.M. The Queen and the Duke of Edinburgh embarked on a
month long tour of Nepal, New Zealand and Australia.

One egg hit Her Majesty and it was the first time in her 34 year
reign that she had been hit by a missile.

At a banquet that same evening The Queen joked that she
preferred her New Zealand eggs from breakfast!

February 18th   1478

Death by drowning

H.R.H. George the Duke of Clarence, brother of King Edward
IV, met his death this day.

Convinced that Clarence was aiming at his throne the King
unfolded charges against him.

Both Houses of Parliament passed the Bill of Attainder, and the
sentence of death was carried out secretly in the Tower of London.

Soon after the event the rumour gained ground that the Duke of
Clarence had been drowned in a butt of malmsey wine, for which
he was known to have a partiality.

February 19th   1960

After 103 years

Prince Andrew was born at Buckingham Palace at 3.30 pm. It was the first time a reigning Sovereign had produced a baby since 1857. He was christened Andrew Albert Christian Edward in the Music Room.

February 20th   1603

The omen of the Coronation Ring

The indestructible Queen Elizabeth was definitely unwell, but throughout February she continued to take part in the Affairs of State. However she commanded the Ring with which at her Coronation she had been joined in marriage to her Kingdom to be taken off.

It had to be filed from her finger because it had grown into the flesh and there was no other way to remove it.

The Court took it as a bad omen that the marriage with her kingdom was now dissolved.

February 21st   1728

Tzar Peter III born at Keil

He was born to Anna, one of Peter the Great's daughters. He was brought to Russia by his aunt Elizabeth shortly before she became Empress.

Soon after his marriage to Catherine he alienated her affections. She suspected that he had plans to divorce her and conspired with her lover Grigory Grigoryevich Orlov to overthrow him.

On July 9th 1762 Catherine, with the approval of the guard, the Senate and the Church, became Catherine II, Empress of Russia.

Tzar Peter was later murdered.

February 22nd   1967

H.M. Queen Margrethe of Denmark

Today H.M. Queen Margrethe became the first Queen regnant of Denmark in six hundred years.

She is extremely clever and had a remarkable all-round education and is a graduate of five Universities.

She met her husband, Count Henri de Laborde de Montpezat in London. He was a polished, handsome young diplomat and the Third Secretary at the French Embassy.

On the day of their marriage Henri became Prince Henrik of Denmark and enjoys the Queen's passion for archaeology and bridge.

Denmark is one of the oldest Kingdoms in Europe and Queen Margrethe loves ruling over it.

"It is no strain," she says "I enjoy doing it. It is a happy duty."

February 23rd   1870

The Prince in the witness box

H.R.H. The Prince of Wales stood in the witness-box, to refute
an accusation of 'undue familiarity' as part of the divorce
proceedings between Lord Mordaunt and his wife, one of the
Beauties of the Marlborough House set.

In the opinion of intelligent men the Prince had done the right
thing to clear himself as much as possible from such an unpleasant
accusation.

However, Queen Victoria was furious.

February 24th   1981

The engagement of the 21st Prince of Wales

The engagement of H.R.H. Charles Prince of Wales to Lady
Diana Spencer had already been forecast by the Press and the
whole Nation approved his choice.

They thought the quiet, shy, sweet gentle girl who loved
children and who had never been written about with any other man
was exactly who they wanted as their future Queen.

It was the most popular engagement in the whole history of the
Royal Family.

February 25th   1601

The Earl of Essex beheaded

H.M. Queen Elizabeth had waited in vain for the arrival of a ring while the Earl was under sentence of death.

It was a ring which she had once given him, and which was a token of his devotion and love.

Had that ring arrived, he would have been saved. In fact Essex despatched the ring with instructions to his messenger to deliver it to the Queen's Chief lady – Lady Scope.

Accidentally it fell into the hands of her sister, the Countess of Nottingham, whose husband was so bitter an enemy of Essex. He made her withhold it from the Queen.

Essex was, therefore, left unpardoned and beheaded. Not until January 1603 did Lady Nottingham confess to Her Majesty what she had done.

It was a death-blow to Queen Elizabeth who died two months later.

February 26th   1815

Napoleon escapes from Elba

The news that Napoleon Bonaparte was moving towards Paris came as a bombshell to the Congress of Vienna which had met the previous September to provide a blue-print for peace in Europe.

The futile Louis XVIII fled to Lille leaving on his desk a secret Treaty against Russia.

Waterloo was fought and Napoleon defeated. This time he was sent to St. Helena.

February 27th   1919

A love marriage

H.R.H. Princess Patricia of Connaught married Commander the Hon. Alexander Ramsey. It was the first recent wedding to be held at Westminster Abbey.

This marriage provided something exciting and charming for the nation after the gruelling years of World War I. The Princess was beautiful and popular.

She relinquished her Royal title and became Lady Patricia Ramsey.

February 28th   1695

A Royal prisoner of love

H.R.H. Princess Sophie Dorothea, Electress of Hanover, grand-daughter of James I and wife of George Lewis, was sent to Ahlden Castle, convicted of adultery.

After their marriage she became appalled by her husband's infidelity. The couple had little in common and soon Sophie Dorothea met the young, handsome and dashing Count Philip Christopher von Konigsmarck.

In 1690 the letters between Konigsmarck and Sophie Dorothea began to flow to each other through her Lady-in-Waiting, but Sophie Dorothea still had her doubts and scruples.

Her position was extremely dangerous and she had experienced her husband's temper a number of times. Once he nearly strangled her.

Eventually, Sophie Dorothea allowed her heart to rule her head. Sometime in the first months of 1691 the liaison was consummated. The letters became even more frequent and Konigsmarck even signed one in blood.

George Lewis found out about them and Konigsmarck vanished, presumably murdered.

Sophie Dorothea remained at Ahlden for thirty-two years until her death.

February 29th   1872

John Brown to the rescue

Eighteen year old Arthur O'Connor fired blanks at Queen Victoria as Her Majesty entered Buckingham Palace. He was caught by John Brown. (He was tried, pleaded guilty and sentenced to imprisonment and flogging – 9th April).

The Queen said later that she was 'terribly alarmed.'

MARCH

March 1st   1902

Unlucky

King Edward VII never sat down thirteen to a meal.

One day he arrived at a friend's house to find they were thirteen, waiting for number fourteen who had not yet arrived.

Time went by and the King grew more and more irritated when suddenly a young Subaltern appeared, whereupon the King turned to him fiercely.

"Why the hell are you so late?"

"I am sorry, Sir," the young Subaltern said, "I did not start soon enough."

The unlucky young Subaltern was Winston Churchill.

March 2nd   1982

The Queen Mother's daffodils

Philip Delaney had moved his store to the village of Prestbury from Leckhampton, where the Queen Mother had always paused to receive from him a gift of flowers and mint chocolates.

Her Majesty had however promised to make a detour to see him.

"I knew if there was a crowd the car would slow down for us," he said "and I was handing out daffodils to the children to wave, when around the corner she came. . . . and continued up the road."

All were reeling with disappointment when the Queen Mother asked her chauffeur to turn back – leaving her police outriders to journey on until they, too, turned back in search of the lost Royal car.

Philip Delaney was still clutching his dripping bunch of daffodils when the door of Her Majesty's limousine opened.

"Oh, Mr. Delaney," the Queen Mother exclaimed "are those flowers for me?"

"Yes, Ma'am," he replied "but I'm sorry they're not properly arranged."

"That's exactly how I love flowers," she smiled.

March 3rd   1808

A step up

On this day, Joachim Murat and Caroline Bonaparte became King and Queen of Naples.

Caroline had fallen madly in love with Murat who was only an inn-keeper's son.

She had met him when she was being fêted by Italian Society and as at that time he had two Mistresses he was not interested in her and she returned to School in France.

Sixteen months later after he had been severely wounded during the Egyptian War he took some notice of Caroline as she was very beautiful.

Caroline again returned to School.

Murat was aiding Napoleon in his effort to oust the Directoire.

After midnight on the night of the Coup, Murat sent four Grenadiers to inform Caroline that her brother was safe and had been appointed First Consul.

March 4th   1975

A Knight in slippers

H.M. Queen Elizabeth II knighted on this day the silent movie
star Charlie Chaplin. *The Times* reported:
"Intimations of farce inseparable from the name of Chaplin
lingered in the air. The music-stand of the Conductor of the
orchestra collapsed with a clatter. Chaplin was wearing impeccable
black morning clothes except for his feet, clad in blue suede
slippers."

March 5th   1902

The King's trick

'Bertie' as King Edward VII was called by the Royal Family
enjoyed the joke at Marlborough House in the Smoking-Room
Library.
In his time there was a secret door which looked like book-cases
full of books but could only be opened when one found the tab
affixed to one of them.
The fake books were entitled in typical Edwardian humour:
*Warm Receptions – by Burns; Lamb on the death of Wolfe; Payne's
Dentistry; Spare That Tree by Y. Hewett,* and so on.
One can imagine King Edward's delight in exhibiting this trick to
his friends.

March 6th   1856

The passionate beauty

On this day Sheikh Abdul Medjeul El Mezrab married the greatest beauty of her day. Jane Digby was irresistible, fascinating, reckless, with eyes that could move a Saint.

It was always said that Jane's love affairs read like a naughty Almanach de Gotha. She married Lord Ellenborough, ran away with Prince Felix Schwarzenberg, had King Ludwig I of Bavaria in love with her and married for the second time Baron Carl Theodore von Venningen, who was young, handsome and rich.

She found him boring and ran away with Count Spyridon Theotoky. There was a duel and the Count was wounded.

Jane's next lover was King Otto of Greece and she caused a great deal of scandal in that country. Then when negotiating for a Camel Caravan to take her across the desert she met the Sheikh.

He was Royal, well educated and spoke several languages and when she looked into his dark eyes, Jane had met her fourth and last husband and the great love of her life.

She was loved and accepted by the tribe as their Queen. She lived in a tent, hunted with Medjeul and waited on him for twenty-five years.

Her marriage was wildly and ecstatically passionate and they remain for ever two of the most exciting and alluring lovers in the whole world.

March 7th   1863

The Alexandra Rose

H.R.H. Princess Alexandra landed at Gravesend, for her marriage to H.R.H. Prince of Wales. The Prince led his fiancée along the Terrace Pier at Gravesend, after she disembarked from the Royal yacht *Victoria and Albert.*

She was accompanied on the voyage by the King and Queen of Denmark and other members of the Danish Royal Family, Officials and Dignitaries.

The Illustrated London News reported:

"A bevy of pretty maids, who, ranged on each side of the pier, awaited, with dainty little baskets filled with spring flowers, the arrival of the Princess, to scatter these, Nature's jewels, at the feet of the Royal Lady."

The Alexandra rose became an emblem of the beautiful bride and jewellers hurried to design them in diamonds set in platinum instead of gold.

March 8th   1796

"And So To Bed"

The Civil Marriage of Napoleon Bonaparte and Josephine Viscountesse de Beauharnais took place to-day.

When Napoleon met Josephine he fell head over heels in love for the first time in his life. He learnt with her the rapturous satisfaction of passion given and received.

He begged Josephine to marry him but she would not name the day.

Then on Wednesday 8th March, a stormy night, the Mayor of the district in which Napoleon lived was got out of bed by a man in the uniform of a General, who told him to perform the Marriage Service immediately.

The Civil Union of the Revolutionary Regime did not take long.

When it was over the Bride and Bridegroom immediately returned to Josephine's house to the same bed where in the past two weeks they had already found a wild, fiery passionate happiness.

March 9th   1774

Behind closed doors

At last H.M. Catherine the Great, Empress of Russia secretly married Prince Gregory Potemkin her lover for many years.

The Empress had taken a number of lovers when Peter her mad husband never consummated the marriage.

She was reviewing her troops when she noticed that the knob of her sword was missing.

A young man rode out of the ranks, presented her with his and fell madly in love with her.

He was tall, dark, fiery, excitable, witty and intelligent but the Empress kept him dangling for a year.

In despair he entered a Monastery.

Catherine who was now forty-four had him brought back and took him as her lover.

He appealed to Catherine's mind as well as her body. Her 357 surviving letters to him show how wildly in love she was.

"My Beloved, I love you greatly, you are handsome, intelligent, amusing . . . I often try to hide my feelings but my heart betrays my passion."

They were secretly married in the Church of St. Sampson on the outskirts of St. Petersburg.

March 10th   1966

Bombs and tear gas

No Bride ever had a more frightening Wedding Day than the Crown Princess Beatrix of the Netherlands on March 10th 1966.

There was an angry march on the Palace. Demonstrations and fighting with the Police. Tear gas clouding the air, protestors smashing windows and destroying cars.

Bombs were thrown at the Golden Coach and there were cries for the Abolition of the Monarchy.

The Dutch people were horrified when Queen Juliana on the Radio and Television informed them in July 1965 that her daughter Beatrix was engaged to Claus von Amsberg.

He had, during the War, worn the hated uniform of the Nazi Wehrmacht and been a member of the Hitler youth.

There were marches, rallies and demonstrations and the crowds shouted: *"Claus raus, Claus raus"*.

The Dutch Press who were mostly pro-Royal, were disturbed.

Few people knew how hard Queen Juliana had tried to prevent the marriage, even attempting to get Claus, a Diplomat, transferred out of Europe.

Princess Beatrix was however deeply in love and had a three-day hunger strike which made her Mother give in.

The marriage took place and love triumphed.

Queen Beatrix and Prince Claus who were blissfully happy together later won the hearts of the Dutch people.

March 11th   1900

Royal Stitches

H.M. King George V's son, David, the Prince of Wales described when he was the Duke of Windsor how as a child:

'No words that I was ever to hear could be so disconcerting – as the summons, usually delivered by a footman: "His Royal Highness wishes to see you in the Library."

King George was so furious when he saw the Prince standing with his hands in his pockets that he ordered the children's Nanny, Mrs. Bill, to sew up the pockets of all the boys' trousers.

March 12th   1801

'Russian wit'

To-day the tall, fair-haired Tzar Alexander I Emperor of Russia aged 24 rode to his Coronation.

A Wit remarked that he was preceded by the man who had murdered his grandfather, escorted by the men who had murdered his father, and followed by the men who would not think twice about murdering him.

March 13th   1910

Odious owls

H.M. King Ferdinand I of Bulgaria was very superstitious on this day as he was on the 13th of each month.

He wore gloves to ward off evil spirits and never did anything that might seem dangerous. He was a naturalist, zoologist and botanist and wrote a standard work on the flora and fauna of Brazil.

He loved birds and had an enormous aviary which contained every known species of birds found in Bulgaria.

That however did not prevent him from being determined ruthlessly to exterminate every owl in his own country. He believed that they were the bringers of bad luck and this in fact, was his most fervent superstition of them all.

March 14th   1590

The fourteenth day

On this day Henry IV of France won the battle of Ivry.

It was not surprising he was the victor as the 14th was his lucky day. He was the fourteenth King of France, had 14 letters to his name, Henri de Bourbon, and his birthday was the 14th May 1553, which incidentally adds up to fourteen.

Besides this his first wife Marguerite de Valois was born on the 14th May 1552, and the Parisians rose in revolt against him on the 14th May 1558, he also had a great military and ecclesiastical demonstration organised against him on the 14th May 1590.

Not unnaturally he was extremely superstitious but he obviously overcame his fears when on the 13th May 1610 he arranged the coronation of his second wife.

It was strange that he should have done this because he was warned that he would not long survive the event.

On the 14th May his heart was pierced by the dagger of an assailant called Ravaillac.

March 15th   1940

A Royal tit bit

An aged Bishop was invited to luncheon and was seated next to Queen Mary.

Her Majesty was living at Badminton House, home of the Duke and Duchess of Beaufort for the duration of the war.

One of the small dogs belonging to the Duchess moved close to the Bishop begging for scraps.

His Grace ignored the animal, but Queen Mary handed him a tough piece of meat she had discarded and said:

"Give this to the little chap".

The Bishop, being rather deaf, took the meat and to the Queen's amazement popped it into his own mouth, chewing valiantly. He imagined the Queen had given him a Royal command!

March 16th   1881

Pomp and ceremony

The Prince of Wales on a visit to St. Petersburg invested the new Tzar with The Order of the Garter.

The Insignia, the star, the ribbon, the collar, the sword and the actual garter itself were all carried on separate long narrow cushions of red velvet, heavily trimmed with gold bullion.

Among those present beside the new Emperor and Empress were the Princess of Wales, the Grand Master and Grand Mistress of the Russian Court, members of the British Embassy, the Prince of Wales and his staff.

As they entered the Throne room, a perfectly audible female voice cried out in English:

"Oh! my dear! Do look at them! They look exactly like a row of wet-nurses carrying babies!"

The Empress and the Princess of Wales looked at each other and exploded with laughter!

March 17th   1965

"The last Pharaoh"

H.M. King Farouk I formerly King of Egypt took his latest mistress Annamaria Gatti to his favourite French restaurant.

45 years of age, the King was very fat weighing almost 20 stone, owing to the fact that he ate chocolates continually, besides large meals.

When they sat down to luncheon he ordered a dozen oysters, Lobster thermidor, had a third helping of Roast lamb, chips and string beans, followed with a huge helping of chestnut trifle and two oranges.

Then he died!

He was the last King of Egypt and the last Pharaoh. He had been deposed by Colonel Nasser in 1952 but he went into exile with a twenty strong retinue.

He left the largest collection of pornography ever known, the greatest stamp collection in the world and an enormous amount of other treasures many of which he had been given, some of which when he liked them he stole as if it was his right.

March 18th   979

The treachery of a Queen

H.M. King Edward I was hunting in the forest of Dorset and, knowing he was in the neighbourhood of Corfe, he left his friends and rode alone to pay a visit to his mother.

Queen Elfrida received him with the warmest demonstrations of affection, and as he was unwilling to dismount from his horse, she offered him a cup of wine with her own hand.

While he was drinking it one of the Queen's attendants, by her command, stabbed him with a dagger.

The King hastily turned his horse, and rode toward the wood, but he became faint and fell from the saddle. His foot was entangled in the stirrup and he was dragged along until the horse was stopped.

The corpse was carried to the cottage of a poor woman, where it was found there the next day and thrown on Queen Elfrida's orders into an adjoining marsh.

It is said:– "No worse deed than this was done to the Anglo race, since they first came to Britain."

March 19th   1986

A tail to tell

An official announcement is made of the engagement between H.R.H. Prince Andrew and Miss Sarah Ferguson.

Prince Andrew had proposed a month earlier in the romantic setting of Floors Castle, the home of the Duke of Roxburgh.

To-day the Press Office at Buckingham Palace sent a young lady to the waiting reporters with a handful of typewritten notices.

In the excitement a copy was seized by an onlooker's old English sheepdog called Peggy, who ran off with it.

Her owner set off in hot pursuit.

March 20th   1963

"Yes, yes, yes!"

H. H. Maharaj Prince Sikkim Palden Thondup Namgyl had 15,000 guests at his wedding in Sikkim.

At the reception, 400 chickens, 100 goats and 200 pigs were needed for the Royal Feast.

The Prince was a widower when he met his future wife in the lounge of a Hotel in Darjeeling in India.

Miss Cooke aged 21 had been in Sikkim to study Oriental languages.

She was American and her family ancestry went back to the 'Mayflower'. Her uncle with whom she lived had been Ambassador in the Netherlands, Panama, Iran and Peru.

After their first meeting Hope and the Prince wrote to each other and she told her American friends "he was a very wise and good man".

The Prince proposed on a dance-floor in 1961. She answered, "Yes, yes, yes!".

To her friends she said: "There was no great design on my part to marry a King. I fell in love with his sad, sad, sad eyes, his smile and his beautifully courteous manners."

Sikkim is a poor country but fortunately Queen Hope contributes to the Royal finances with her large fortune.

March 21st   1818

A happy Marriage

When the marriage between H.R.H. The Duke of Clarence and Princess Adelaide of Saxe-Meiningen was arranged the Duke did not know whether to be more sorry for himself or for his bride.

He was 52, she was 25.

"She is doomed, poor dear innocent young creature, to be my wife," he wrote disconsolately. "I cannot, I will not, I must not ill use her . . ."

Both parties good-natured and anxious to please, were determined to make a success of it. Yet it still caused surprise when the marriage proved an instant, total and lasting success.

The Prince Regent, who called on them two days after the wedding, found them 'sitting by the fire exactly like Darby and Joan'.

The Duke of Clarence was an amorous roué with ten illegitimate children. But as King William IV he became exceedingly reputable and inevitably excessively dull.

March 22nd

H.R.H. Prince Edwold becomes a Saint

The brother of King Edmund of East Anglia had become fed up with bowing at Court and of blind obedience to the Monarch.

He renounced his Royal life, his title, and became a hermit.

His cell was on the top of a hill in Dorset and he lived there sustained by nothing but bread and water until his death. After which he became known as Saint Edwold.

March 23rd 1943

A Royal break down

Queen Mary and her Lady of the Bedchamber, Lady Desborough, were driving from Badminton to Oxford with the University's Chancellor. Unfortunately their car broke down. Owing to wartime shortage of petrol there was little traffic on the country road.

The first vehicle to pass was a small car in which sat a farmer, his wife and a load of onions. Readily agreeing to transport the Queen to her engagement in Oxford, the farmer moved his onions to the back seat, while the Queen joined him in the front.

His wife and Lady Desborough spent the rest of the journey seated on top of the high-smelling onions.

March 24th 1603

H.M. Queen Elizabeth dies at Richmond Palace

Nobody could persuade her to see her physicians and having performed her last duty by nominating James as her successor, she centred her mind on Heavenly things, rejoicing in the ministrations of her spiritual physician, her "black husband", Archbishop Whitgift.

Then she turned her face to the wall, and sank into a stupor and between the hours of two and three in the morning passed quietly away, 'as the most resplendent sun setteth at last in a western cloud.'

March 25th   1875

An embarrassed King

H.R.H. The Prince of Wales came to spend to-day at Mello with the Princesse de Sagan.

The Sagan son aged 15, heir to the most illustrious French title, had developed violent feelings concerning his mother's love affair with the Prince of Wales.

The young man, entering her Boudoir, saw His Royal Highness's clothes on a chair.

He snatched them up and ran out of the French window to hurl the bundle into the huge water fountain.

When the Prince emerged from the Princesse's bedroom it was to find his sopping apparel being dragged from the goldfish by hysterical servants.

Understandably the Prince was annoyed as he had to leave in borrowed trousers which were too tight.

But he took the situation bravely as an Englishman should.

March 26th   1719

A Dresden drama

To everyone's astonishment H.R.H. Prince Augustus of Saxony marries a dwarf.

His father was a man of good taste who made Dresden the most civilised City in the world and a haven of lovely women.

Prince Augustus was more interested in pictures than power and his passion for the Arts was even greater than his father's.

Although he adored beauty he fell madly in love with the clever, fascinating, excessively lovely dwarf – the Archduchess Maria Josepha.

He married her in Vienna but when the happy couple arrived in Dresden his father thought a very pretty Lady-in-Waiting was the Bride and kissed her with paternal fervour.

After he learnt he had made a mistake he consoled the pretty Lady-in-Waiting for not being his daughter-in-law by making her his mistress.

March 27th   1625

A Royal stroke

H.M. King James I had suffered a stroke three days earlier and was conscious although speechless before he died.

During his reign there was a gibbet, a fire, and a torture chamber ready everywhere 'for the agents of Satan'.

The Act of Parliament passed in his reign made it punishable by death to conjure up or remove an evil spirit or to injure cattle by means of charms.

March 28th   1571

A costly drink

Sultan Selim I of the Ottoman Empire was known as 'Selim the
Sot'. His red face and large stomach were due to him being
permanently drunk.

Unlike most alcoholics, however, he was very particular about
what he drank, and most of all he liked Cyprus wine.

He was extremely upset when he discovered that his stocks of this
particular wine were getting low, and he decided to invade the
island.

The Turks sacked Nicosia, massacred 30,000 islanders and then
besieged the fortress of Famagusta for two years. It was the most
expensive wine ever produced.

It was also the death of the Sultan. One day, after drinking a
whole bottle of it, he staggered off for a bath, slipped on the marble
floor, broke his skull and died.

March 27th   1972

The curse of Tutankhamun

H.M. The Queen opened the Tutankhamun exhibition at the
British Museum to-day to mark the 50th Anniversary of the
sensational discovery of the tomb.

It was during the reign of Her Majesty's grandfather, King George
V, that Howard Carter entered the tomb of the boy King. The
Queen thanked the Egyptian people "for allowing these priceless
heirlooms to come to London."

She spoke of the "thrill" that Howard Carter and the Earl of Carnarvon must have felt as they entered the tomb.

The curse which was laid on those who visited the tomb was for the moment forgotten. The Earl of Carnarvon had a small mosquito bite. He thought nothing of it but obviously he had blood poisoning.

He died suddenly at 2 o'clock in the afternoon and at the moment he passed away all the lights in Cairo went out for five minutes.

The Egyptians were quite certain it was on the orders of King Tut. The Electricity Board could find no explanation whatsoever of the occurrence.

March 30th   1566

Battle for a gown

Queen Elizabeth gave one of her Maids of Honour, Mary Howard, a dress of purple velvet lined with satin and taffeta. She frequently gave gifts of clothes to her ladies but on one occasion was forced to turn the tables.

Lady Mary Howard, who had no fear of the Queen, went so far as to rival her Majesty for the Earl of Essex. To attract his attention Lady Mary bought herself one of the finest dresses ever seen at a Court renowned for its high fashion.

Queen Elizabeth was furious to be so out-done and one day in Lady Mary's absence stole the dress. She paraded in it and asked her

Lady in Waiting if it were not becoming. Sulkily the girl replied that the gown was too short.

'Why then,' retorted the Queen, 'if it become not me as being too short, I am minded it shall never become you as being too fine; it fitteth neither well.'

Lady Mary put away her dress and it was taken out only after the Queen was safely dead. But by then the Earl had been beheaded.

March 31st   1883

Death of John Brown

King Leopold of the Belgiums (who was to die exactly one year later whilst on holiday with his wife at Cannes) broke the news of John Brown's death to Queen Victoria. John Brown had caught a chill some days earlier but failed to recover.

Queen Victoria wrote in her journal:

"It is the loss not only of a servant but of a real friend. He protected me so, was so powerful and strong – that I felt so safe! And now all, all is gone in this world and all seems unhinged again in thousands of ways!"

In 1865 Queen Victoria had decided that the brusque Scotsman should become a permanent member of the household as 'The Queen's Highland Servant.'

His responsibilities increased although he was disliked by most Members of the Royal Family and staff.

APRIL

April 1st

A Royal April fool

Among all the Courtiers who surrounded Charles II, none was more celebrated for his conviviality and wit than the Earl of Rochester.

He himself confessed that for five years he was never sober. On one occasion, he scribbled on King Charles's bedroom door a mock epitaph:

'Here lies our Sovereign Lord the King,
  Whose word no man relies on;
Who never says a foolish thing,
  Nor ever does a wise one.'

He joined King Charles in many of his wild pranks in the streets of London and he could impersonate any character to perfection.

April 2nd   1502

His Widow married his brother

Arthur, Prince of Wales, son of Henry VII, died at Ludlow Castle. He had recently married Catherine of Aragon, aged 15, to whom he was engaged when she was three.

The untimely death of this amiable and charming Prince caused great grief.

Henry VII for political reasons, and on the plea that the marriage had never been consummated, married the widow of Arthur to his younger brother Henry, who was 18 and the future King Henry VIII.

April 3rd   1900

The Prince of Wales saved by – HAIR

When Edward Prince of Wales and Princess Alexandra were on a state visit to Brussels, Miss Charlotte Knollys, a lady-in-waiting, accompanied them.

As she sat with them in their train at the Gare du Nord a fifteen-year-old anarchist named Sipido aimed a shot at the Prince.

The bullet missed, lodging itself in the bun of hair on Charlotte's head. It was treasured for years afterwards and is still preserved in the Windsor Archives.

April 4th   1581

Rise Sir Francis

HRH Queen Elizabeth knighted Francis Drake today aboard his ship *The Golden Hind* at Deptford.

Recorded in one of the day books of the Wardrobe of Robes is the Queen's loss of two pieces of gold from a black velvet cap.

She also lost a garter of purple and gold which was found by the French Ambassador. Her Majesty later returned it to him as fair prize.

He in turn sent it to the Duke of Alencon who was hoping he could marry the Queen.

April 5th   1933

A Royal tribute

H.M. King George V was delighted with Elizabeth, his daughter-in-law, and writes to his son 'Bertie', the Duke of York:

"The better I know and the more I see of your dear little wife, the more charming I think she is and everyone falls in love with her . ."

The King made allowances for the Duchess that were denied his own children. Her timekeeping was a little erratic and when she arrived two minutes late for dinner the King merely said:

"You are not late, my dear. I think we sat down two minutes early."

When someone criticised her for bad timekeeping the King said:

"If she weren't late, she would be perfect, and how horrible that would be."

April 6th   1199

Death of a great hero

H.R.H. King Richard the Lion Heart dies at the age of forty-two. It was his impetuosity that brought him to his death.

The Vicomte of Limoges refused to hand over a hoard of gold unearthed by a local peasant. King Richard laid siege to his Castle of Chalus and in an unlucky moment was fatally wounded.

He was buried in the Abbey Church of Fontevrault in France where his effigy can still be found.

April 7th   1930

Reincarnated

The Maharajah of Kapurthala like all Indian Princes believed in reincarnation or what is called in the East 'Rebirth'.

He was sure that he was the reincarnation of Louis XIV. He was so convinced of this that he hired a French Architect to build on his land in the foothills of the Himalayas, a complete replica of the Palace of Versailles.

Designers and experts from France came to India to make sure that the fixtures and fittings of the Palace were exactly reproduced.

When the Palace was finished the Maharajah insisted on French being spoken at his Court and he engaged a Cordon Bleu Chef from Paris.

His Sikh servants were made to abandon their traditional turban in favour of powdered wigs and they also wore silk coats, breeches and buckled shoes of the correct seventeenth-century dress.

April 8th   1795

A doomed wedding

The Prince of Wales, later King George IV marries Princess Caroline of Brunswick in the Chapel Royal at St. James's.

Before the ceremony the Prince remarked gloomily to the Duke of Clarence:

"William, tell Mrs. Fitzherbert that she is the only woman I shall ever love."

On his way to the Chapel he said to the Earl of Moira, who was sitting opposite him in the coach:

"It's no use Moira, I shall never love any woman but Fitzherbert."

Neither of these men knew that he had secretly married Mrs. Fitzherbert on 21st December 1785.

The Bride, whose rich dress was so heavy that she almost fell over it, was led into the Chapel by the Duke of Clarence.

She stood at the Altar as she awaited the arrival of the Bridegroom chatting with gusto to the Duke of Clarence.

When the Prince of Wales came supported by the Dukes of Bedford and Roxburgh, he appeared to be extremely nervous and agitated. He had obviously been drinking.

The Prince's drunkenness increased over the day and he was in a bad state when night approached.

When he did eventually make his way into his Bride's bedroom he fell insensible into the fireplace where she left him so he remained there all night.

In the morning he had recovered sufficiently to climb into bed with her.

April 9th   1672

A brave priest

The great Harbinger responsible for finding accommodation when H.M. King Charles II and his Suite travelled, asked the Prebendry of Winchester Cathedral to vacate his house for Nell Gwynn.

The Priest's man refused saying:

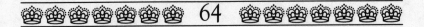

"A woman of ill repute should not be entertained in the house of a Clergyman."

He was threatened and told he could not refuse such a request, thereupon the sagacious Priest got a local builder to remove the roof.

When Nell heard what had happened she laughed until the tears ran down her cheeks.

The King too was amused and also impressed by the Cleric's adherence to his principles.

Later when His Majesty was asked to name a Clergyman for the Bishopric of Bath and Wells, he laughed and exclaimed:

"Odds fish! Who shall have it but that little black fellow who would not give poor Nell a lodging."

April 10th   1535

The Queen is dead

H.M. King Henry VIII ordered the cleaning up and refurbishing of Westminster Abbey.

While this was being done the body of H.M. King Henry V's wife, Catherine de Valois, was dug up.

Her mummified corpse was put on show, and remained accessible to visitors until 1776. Samuel Pepys, the great diarist, on his thirty-sixth birthday paid the verger a shilling to view the Queen.

He recorded:

"I had the upper part of her body in my hands, and I did kiss her mouth, reflecting that it was the first time I did kiss a Queen."

April 11th   1542

Ghost of a Queen

The ghost of Queen Catherine Howard, H.M. King Henry VIII's fifth wife, was heard for the first time today.

Catherine had been beheaded on His Majesty's orders on Tower Green in February.

Before this Queen Catherine was at Hampton Court Palace and escaped from the room in which she was being held prisoner, pending her removal to the Tower.

She ran along the gallery to plead with King Henry who was celebrating Mass in the Chapel. She was chased and held by the guard, and carried back to her room.

As she was dragged along she gave a piercing scream which was heard all over the Palace and would certainly have been heard by the King.

He paid no attention and continued with his Devotions.

Over the succeeding years the shadowy figure of a woman in a billowing white gown has been seen to approach the door leading to the Royal Pew. She tries to open it but suddenly uttering a blood-curdling scream she vanishes.

April 12th   1810

H.M. George III: mad, sane or a little peculiar?

H.M. George III, King of England, has been depicted in literature as being completely mad. He was for some years, however, a kind, caring and hard-working King until he suffered some strange delusions.

He believed that beef grew like vegetables and tried to prove the point by planting 4 lb. of Prime Beef in Windsor Castle's kitchen garden.

For some time he insisted on ending every sentence with the word 'Peacock' and declared that he could see Germany from his Castle bedroom.

April 13th   1914

Thirteen is unlucky

Queen Mary and King George V visited France. Luncheon on board the train bound for Paris was at a long table in the dining car, set with thirteen places.

The Queen firmly announced that she would not eat with a party numbering thirteen. A way out was sought. Someone suggested that if one of the ladies present was pregnant, she could count as two. No lady could oblige.

At length the Royal doctor, Sir James Reid, tactfully announced that he did not wish to have any luncheon and departed from the scene.

April 14th   1630

A surprise pie

H.M. King Charles's wife Queen Henrietta Maria attended a huge Banquet where she was presented with a pie.

From it leaps a dwarf called Jeffrey Hudson who was only 18 inches tall. The Queen was delighted as she liked having dwarfs as servants.

April 15th   1900

No time for Vesuvius

On a Mediterranean cruise His Majesty King Edward VII Queen Alexandra and her sister the Empress Marie, decided to visit Vesuvius.

The King elected to stay behind in the little train, wisely refusing to entrust his bulky person to a donkey.

The Empress, the Queen and Sir Henry Ponsonby who was accompanying them mounted their beasts, the two Royal ladies being given the best donkeys.

They went ahead, and Sir Henry, trailing far behind, suddenly heard the whistle of the train's engine.

King Edward was growing impatient.

Sir Henry urged his donkey forward to catch up and tried to make Her Majesty turn back.

She merely remarked that it was foolish to turn back when half-way there and continued the ascent.

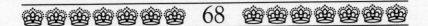

The whistle sounded again and again, each time more shrilly.

Frantic Sir Henry set off and somehow managed to persuade the sisters to return to the train. On his miserable donkey he came in a poor third.

The Monarch's wrath at being kept waiting fell on his innocent head.

April 16th   1673

A child bride

"I do not believe," King Charles II once told the French Ambassador, "there are two men who love women more than you and I do, but my brother, James, devout as he is, loves them more."

When King James's wife Anne Hyde died, he fell head over heels in love with Lady Belasyse, a seventeen-year-old widow of no great beauty and went so far as to propose marriage.

His brother, King Charles, however, would have none of it and with some embarrassment the lady had to agree that the offer was withdrawn.

King Charles and his Statesmen eventually selected the Princess of Modena, only fifteen at the time, when King James was forty. Moreover Princess Mary Beatrice was a Roman Catholic and had intended to take the veil.

His Holiness the Pope, however, persuaded her that marriage to the heir to the Throne of Britain was more important.

The bride and bridegroom were married by proxy without having seen each other, an arrangement hurried on partly to forestall the outcry there would be when Parliament met.

When the child-bride arrived in England they were, as King James himself put it, "married and bedded that same night".

Actually James could not have chosen a better bride for himself. Mary Beatrice was to grow into a woman of striking beauty and in spite of her husband's immoral behaviour, she was to show considerable loyalty to him and at the same time give him love and affection.

April 17th   1863

A duel over a handsome Prince

Cora Pearl, who was English, rose to be one of the most famous Courtesans of the Second Empire.

She aroused the interest of a handsome Prince from the Serbian Royal Family. Unfortunately, another Courtesan Marthe de Vere, also wanted him.

They fought a duel in the Bois with riding whips. Using them freely, both women's faces were so damaged that they could not appear in public for a week:– during which time their Adonis vanished!

April 18th   1340

'Ich Dien – I serve'

King John I of Bohemia lost the sight of one eye in a skirmish against the Lithuanians in 1336 and due to incompetent medical treatment he lost the sight of his other eye in 1340. Yet this did not

deter him from hurling himself into the midst of the fighting at the Battle of Crecy.

When the British and the French faced each other in 1340 the 50 year old warrior was helped into his armour, mounted on his horse and led into the battle.

He died the only way he would have wished to die. The Black Prince was so impressed by his valour that he adopted King John's three-feathered emblem and his motto "*Ich Dien*" as his own.

They have been used by all the Princes of Wales ever since.

April 19th   1881

H.M. The Queen understands

Lord Beaconsfield – the brilliant, witty Disraeli died. The Government wanted to give him a public funeral and burial in Westminster Abbey.

Her Majesty the Queen was consulted. She knew how Dizzy suffered when his beloved wife Mary Anne died nine years earlier.

She had seen the letter 'Dizzy' found after her death. It was dated June 5th 1856.

"My own dear Husband. If I should depart this life before you, leave orders that we may be buried in the same grave at whatever distance you may die from England. And now God Bless you, my kindest, dearest! You have been a perfect husband to me. Be put by my side in the same grave. And now farewell, my dear Dizzy. Do not live alone, dearest. Some one I earnestly hope you may find as attached to you as your own devoted – Mary Anne."

Her Majesty herself knew what love was. She agreed with the Executors that his place was a Hughenden, beside Mary Anne.

April 20th   1956

A magnificent Princess

On this day H. S. H. Prince Rainier of Monaco and his wife the former film star Grace Kelly started their honeymoon and gave a sigh of relief.

The wedding which took place at Monte Carlo the previous day was the greatest ballyhoo of the century.

Never had there been so many reporters, photographers, and sight-seers among the crowds which attended the marriages.

It was a love match which strengthened during the years and was very different from the turbulent marriages and dramatic reigns of the Prince's Grimaldi ancestors, who date back to the eleventh century.

There was so much magic about Monaco that it was only right that the most magical Princess who grew more beautiful every year should reign over that tiny kingdom.

Her charm and her intelligence became a model of Royal dignity which was admired by the whole of Europe.

April 21st   1805

One flaw

The Princess Pauline Borghese, the favourite sister of the Emperor Napoleon, was acclaimed in this year as having the classic beauty of a goddess.

She bathed in milk, and had a negro carry her to the bath so that she could appreciate the whiteness of her skin.

Her only flaw was a badly shaped ear which she hid with her hand when Canova was sculpting her in the nude. She pursued any man she desired and designed the liveries of her footmen in Haiti so as to reveal their masculinity.

She declared that her husband, Prince Borghese, was impotent, (which was untrue) and had tempestuous affairs with members of her brother's staff.

Yet she was the only loyal member of Napoleon's family to visit him on Elba, and helped him in exile on St. Helena.

April 22nd   1738

A bonnet for the Bridegroom

The 15th Prince of Wales, Frederick Lewis was married to Augusta of Saxe-Gotha in the Chapel of St. James's Palace.

The Prince in his youth was allowed to run wild and mingle with ruffians. He attended the local schools, but did not have access to important local scholars.

Strange though it may seem, the fourth mistress he acknowledged was the same Madame D'Elitz who had carried on liaisons both with his father and grandfather.

George Hervey described the wedding night:

"When they were in bed everyone passed through the bedchamber to see them."

The bride was very shy and Queen Charlotte released her stays and guided her to the marriage couch.

The Bridegroom, Frederick, joined Augusta wearing his nightshirt and a high lace cap. His mother sneered at his cap, calling it a 'Grenadier's Bonnet'.

But Augusta must have liked it, because she subsequently gave him nine children.

April 23rd   1913

Undefeated love

Today Princess Indira, only daughter of the progressively minded, saintly Maharaja Sayaji Rao of Baroda was married to H. H. the Maharaja of Cooch Behar.

They were married in a Register Office and then with Brahmo rites in the Buckingham Palace Hotel. It seemed impossible that they would ever find happiness.

Handsome, poetic, eight years older than the bride, Jitendra was the second son of the Maharaja of Cooch Behar a controversial family of a different faith to the Barodas.

Indira secretly sent a letter to him telling him that she was to be betrothed to another Maharaja who she had met in 1911 when her parents took her to the Coronation of H.M. King George V.

Somehow she managed to avoid being married and there were just a few stolen meetings, notes, tears – but little more for the next two years, with the man she loved.

They planned to elope but were discovered and Indira was guarded everywhere she went while her parents would not speak to her.

Then when they were in St. Moritz her father learnt that Jitendra's brother after two years on the throne, was dying in England.

The Barodas gave in and Indira married her love and of course, lived happily ever afterwards.

April 24th   1066

An ill omen from the sky

On Monday, 24th April 1066 what was later to be known as Halley's Comet became visible in the path of the sun.

A scene from the Bayeux Tapestry shows an Astrologer telling King Harold this strange star with a fiery tail was an omen of misfortune.

Six months later King Harold was killed during the Battle of Hastings.

April 25th   1818

The Emperor of Russia orders an egg

Alexander II Emperor of Russia was an extremely mean man. He economised on food, drink, his own clothes, and scolded his wife on the amount she spent on hers. The only extravagance he permitted himself was buying jewellery.

Every year he ordered an Easter Egg, from Peter Carl Fabergé, a Russian of French descent.

Fabergé had set up his workshops in St. Petersburg and all together he made fifty-six jewelled eggs for the Imperial Family, each a masterpiece of ingenuity.

Most of them had shells that opened and inside might be flowers, jewelled figures or enamelled birds that wobbled and flapped their wings.

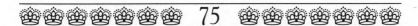

April 26th   1923

Tribute to the fallen

Albert Duke of York, 2nd son of George V, to be George VI, married Lady Elizabeth Bowes-Lyon to-day.

Just after 11 am Lady Elizabeth left her father's house, number 17, Bruton Street, where Princess Elizabeth was to be born, and rode in a State Landau with an escort of four mounted police, to Westminster Abbey.

Before proceeding up the aisle with her father and six bridesmaids, the Bride laid her bouquet upon the Unknown Warrior's grave.

Later on the way to the wedding reception the bride and bridegroom halted at the Cenotaph.

April 27th   703

Brave until the last

The Romans led by General Hassan in Tunis had sworn to bring the Queen Kahena to her knees and on this day the Queen realised she was defeated. She had fought valiantly when they invaded Tunis and united a number of the tribes so that they had forgotten their mutual rivalry and followed her.

She had led them in revolt to Carthage and won a resounding battle. El Djem the famous Colosseum became her headquarters and was turned into a fortress.

Queen Kahena was renowned for her beauty and became more and more powerful through a series of successful campaigns always returning to El Djem in triumph.

Yet the Queen's fortune changed when the General brought his forces against hers. She suffered defeat after defeat but she still retained El Djem.

When her forces could no longer hold out they begged her to go into hiding.

When all was lost, rather than be captured, on this day she plunged her own sword into her breast.

The general, not appeased by this dramatic gesture, cut off her head. He sent it in a basket studded with jewels as a token of fidelity to the Caliph of Baghdad.

April 28th   1654

"What did you say?"

H. K. John IV King of Portugal had the strangest throne in the whole of Europe.

He was extremely deaf and found it infuriating to have to keep saying "What?" to everything that was said to him.

He therefore invented a large and comfortable armchair which he made into a hearing aid. Courtiers wishing to speak to the King would shout their message into an opening of the throne's hollow arms.

The sounds would reverberate along a flexible tube which the King held to his ear to receive the sounds from a trumpet like ending.

April 29th   1694

Augustus the Strong

Today the strong and amazing H.M. Augustus I became King of Saxony.

Of all the Monarchs of the Baroque period, none had been the equal of Augustus.

He was big, tall, with thick black eyebrows and dark eyes and his physical strength was fantastic.

To impress his dinner guests, he would pick up two of his State trumpeters, one in each hand, and hold them at arm's length for five minutes while they played a fanfare.

He kept a harem of beautiful women and when he died he left 354 bastards. It was so difficult for him to keep track of his love children that at least two of his daughters subsequently became his mistresses.

He was able to eat and drink without getting fat and was called "The Ever-cheerful Man of Sin" and "Gay eupeptic son of Belial".

April 30th   1851

A Royal embarrassment

A spectacular, exciting event in H.M. Queen Victoria's married life was the Great Exhibition; Prince Albert had played a vital part in its organisation.

The day before the opening Queen Victoria wrote in her diary:

"Everyone is occupied with the great day. . . . . and my poor Albert is terribly fagged."

The opening went very well and the Queen visited the Exhibition over forty times. On one occasion a highly nervous engraver was showing her a sample of his work which appears to have anticipated Picasso. It portrayed a boy jumping out of a boat watched by a large eye.

Naturally curious, the Queen asked what it meant. The reply was startling.

"The boy, Madam, is the Prince of Wales and the eye is the Eye of God looking out with pleasure for the moment when His Royal Highness will land on his Kingdom and become the reigning Sovereign!"

MAY

May 1st   1625

A Royal proxy marriage

Charles I's marriage to-day to Henrietta Maria (King Henry IV's daughter) at Notre Dame was by proxy.

King Louis XIII "looking like the glorious sun outshining the other stars" escorted his sister to the Cathedral.

Henrietta Maria wore a wedding dress of gold and silver cloth covered with diamonds and precious stones, embroidered with fleur-de-lis.

At the great west door of Notre Dame she was wed to the Duke of Chevreuse acting as Charles's proxy.

Since the Duke was a Huguenot he waited outside the Cathedral for two hours as the French Royal family took nuptial mass.

Afterwards everyone returned to the Archbishop of Paris's Palace for a Wedding Breakfast of 'unmeasured splendour.'

May 2nd   1613

Queen Anne has a shock

Since the death of her son, Prince Henry, Queen Anne's health had seriously deteriorated. Parting from her only daughter further increased her low spirits.

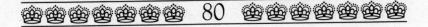

On her doctor's advice she decided to visit Bath to try the beneficial effects of the mineral springs. Her treatment, however, suffered an unfortunate setback before she had time to feel the benefit.

She was in 'The King's Bath' when suddenly 'a flame of fire like a candle. . . . . spread into a large circle on top of the water.' The Queen was terrified.

Being superstitious, she believed the light to be 'a supernatural message from the world below and nothing would induce her to enter The King's Bath again.'

To the annoyance of the Municipal Authorities the Queen insisted on using the new bath, which had been built for the poor people of the town, and they never regained the use of it.

May 3rd   1873

A Royal tit-for-tat

His Imperial Highness the *Duc* d'Aumale was President of the *Conseil* at the trial of Marshal Bazaine who during the Franco-Prussian War had surrendered at Metz.

Leonide Leblanc, a famous Courtesan known as *Mademoiselle Maximum* for the amount of her lovers was among the spectators in the Courtroom when a Society woman complained that she had taken her seat.

"I am dining with *Monseigneur* this evening," she stormed, "and I shall complain to him about this affront."

"Ah! so you are dining with him," Leonide replied imperturbably. "I am having supper and sleeping with him."

May 4th   1920

H.R.H. The Prince of Wales on his tour of New Zealand

The Hunt Valley people threw more confetti than anyone else on the visit.

One girl threw the entire box which broke, pouring its contents down the Prince's neck, to his great annoyance.

May 5th   1802

From Corporal to Consul

Napoleon Bonaparte the First Consul is reviewing his troops outside the Tuileries. Fanny Burney described him as having a 'deeply impressive face'.

He had also learnt to live in an impressive style. He used the Louis XVI suite of eight rooms on the first floor of the Palace. He was waited on by servants in the pale blue livery decorated with silver lace.

He and Josephine slept in a double bed of mahogany, heavily ornamented with ormolu in a draped recess.

He adored steaming hot baths, shaved himself with razors from England which had mother of pearl handles and to finish his toilet his Valet poured eau de cologne over his head and down to his waist.

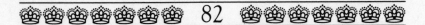

May 6th   1910

A much loved Monarch

H.M. King Edward VII had been clearly unwell for six days but refused to give in. On the morning of May 6th he insisted on dressing to receive his old friend Sir Ernest Cassel but that he could only manage to smoke half a cigar was considered by his household as a bad sign.

In the afternoon it was announced that the King's Filly 'Witch of the Air' had won a race at Kempton Park. When His Majesty was told he murmured: "I am very glad". They were his last recorded words.

When he died every type and age of person in the country mourned their King. One lady who often entertained him threaded black ribbon through her small daughter's underwear.

At the Monarch's very impressive funeral May, daughter of Princess Alexandra of Texk exclaimed: "Why is Uncle Bertie in a box?"

The small daughter of Lord Kinnoull who had witnessed the procession refused to say her prayers, saying:

"It won't be any use, God will be too busy unpacking King Edward."

May 7th   1724

Tsar Peter the Emperor of Russia crowns his wife Catherine

The Nation was aghast. A woman had never been crowned before and it was an outrage.

The Tsarina Catherine had borne eleven children and had supported him through every difficulty and horror of his reign.

But some weeks later Tsar Peter accused her of having an affair with one of her Courtiers, the handsome unscrupulous William Moors who had been accepting huge bribes.

Moors was arrested and beheaded. The Tsar preserved his head in spirits and put it in his wife's bedroom.

May 8th   1945

V. E. Day at Buckingham Palace

After almost six years of unparalleled suffering, terror and desperate resistance, there was no limit to the nation's relief and jubilation at Britain's victory in the Second World War on the surrender of Germany.

Multitudes gathered outside Buckingham Palace on VE Day, loyally cheering their King. At night floodlights were switched on and again and again the Royal Family stepped on to the balcony at the demand of an exultant crowd.

A secret for many years was that Princesses Elizabeth and Margaret with a group of friends slipped out of the Trade Gate at Buckingham Palace to join the throng. Unrecognised, they swept along with the revellers and quickly separated from the two policemen guarding them.

Never before had the two next in succession to the throne mixed so freely amongst the people.

"I think it was one of the most memorable days of my life," said Princess Elizabeth.

That night the King wrote sadly in his diary of his two daughters: "Poor darlings, they have never had any fun yet."

May 9th   1670

Nell Gwyn gives birth to a boy

The triumphant success of the orange girl at Drury Lane had delighted the theatre-lovers.

Yet just before the opening of the expensive production *The Conquest of Granada* she disappeared.

"Nell's with the King," everyone whispered.

She was back again in the Autumn – the same trim little figure and the same elfin humour.

She had captivated the King with her beauty and her Cockney. He loved her more than he loved any of his other women.

Nell was so different when the mob hurled stones at the Royal Coach, thinking it contained the King's French mistress, who they hated. Nell popped her head out of the window and said:

"Pray, good people, be silent. I'm the Protestant whore."

Later the King made her son the Duke of St Albans.

May 10th   1629

A tragedy for the Royal line

H.M. Charles I had fallen deeply in love with his Queen Henrietta Maria, after they were married. He remained faithful to her to the end of his life, a phenomenon unheard of amongst the Monarchs of the seventeenth century.

Apart from King Charles being beheaded his first-born son, Charles, Duke of Cornwall, arrived prematurely and lived only just long enough to be baptized.

It happened because there was a dog-fight between two large hounds which frightened the Queen, and she was also jolted when landing from her barge at Greenwich.

King Charles was the only British King ever to be beheaded by his subjects.

May 11th   1935

The King and Queen astonished

H.M. King George and Queen Mary rested after the excitement of the Silver Jubilee. They looked back with surprise and bewilderment.

From the moment they left Buckingham Palace to drive to St. Pauls, King George was astounded by the enthusiasm of the crowds.

"I had no idea they felt like that about me," he exclaimed wonderingly. "I am beginning to think that they must really like me for myself."

When they reached the City, Queen Mary was in tears.

May 12th   1937

God save the King

The Coronation of H.M. King George VI and H.M. Queen
Elizabeth took place on the date chosen for the Coronation of
Edward VIII, but after the abdication it was decided to go ahead
and crown George VI.

The Queen wrote to the Archbishop of Canterbury:

"I can hardly now believe that we have been called to this
tremendous task . . . the curious thing is that we are not afraid. I
feel that God has enabled us to face the situation calmly."

At the Ceremony the Queen wore the Crown in which was the
most magnificent gem, the legendary Koh-i-noor diamond of 108
carats.

It had belonged to the Mogul Queen Mumtaz Mahal in whose
memory the Taj Mahal was built. The diamond must be worn by a
woman because to a man it would bring certain disaster.

May 13th   1515

Love wins

Today H.M. Mary, Queen of France married her lover for the
second time. There was a national outcry in 1515 when it was
known that the beautiful young Mary Tudor, exquisitely graceful
sister of Henry VIII, was to marry broken-down, toothless Louis
XII.

She had however consented to the alliance only when her brother promised that she should marry the Duke of Suffolk, whom she loved, as soon as the King died.

He conveniently did so eleven weeks after the marriage.

There was however a threat from Louis's lascivious nephew and successor and another from Henry VIII, who wanted Mary to marry the ugliest, most powerful ruler in Europe, the Archduke Charles.

"I would rather be torn in pieces," Mary cried.

The Duke of Suffolk, who adored her, cast prudence to the winds and married her secretly, knowing he might be beheaded.

King Henry was furious but Mary was his favourite sister and by the time the lovers reached England his anger had cooled.

He then insisted their union should be publicly solemnised at Greenwich on the 13th May 1515 in his presence and that of the entire Court.

May 14th   1514

The King of Hearts

Francois I, builder of Blois and Chambord, the host of the Field of Cloth of Gold, restorer of Fontainebleau, married Claude de France, Duchess of Brittany.

She was very small, strangely fat, walked with a limp and had a marked squint. However Francois was fond of her because she was charming, kind, and a good mother.

He, being handsome, gallant, full of grace and Majesty had many beautiful women in love with him. He had his first sexual adventure

at the age of fifteen and began to enjoy women in two ways – on a purely sensual level, and aesthetically. He regarded them as a work of art.

His sister was always his ideal woman. "She had the beauty of a woman, the heart of a man and the head of an angel." Francois was in turn, her idol.

The King's sexual adventures were the talk of his own Court and of Europe where his harem was known as *"la petite bande"*.

May 15th   1876

Red hair in the sunlight

Queen Maria Pia of Savoy, wife of Louis I commissioned on this day a diadem of Diamond Stars.

Beautiful, whimsical, smart and a spendthrift, she was very popular.

One day, wearing the diadem, she had the *Te Deum* in Lisbon Cathedral delayed by half-an-hour so that the sunshine coming through the stained glass windows should fall at an angle on her red hair the moment she entered the Sanctuary.

May 16th   1897

A Court actress

Sarah Bernhardt, who was staying at the same hotel as Queen Victoria at Cimiez near Nice, performed at her own request, in the Queen's Drawing Room.

Queen Victoria wrote in her journal:
"It is extremely touching, and Sarah Bernhardt's acting was quite marvellous, so pathetic and full of feeling."

May 17th   1945

Cheers for the King

H.M. King George VI arrived on the Normandy beaches nine days after D-Day to meet 3,000 British soldiers.

As the King walked out onto the verandah of the villa, first one man, then another recognised him. As if called by one voice thousands of men, most of them semi-nude, many of them still dripping with water, raced up the beach like a human wave.

Then as if the wave had suddenly frozen, they stood silently below the verandah, a solid mass of tanned and dripping men. There was one of those strange silences one sometimes gets among a crowd.

Then a voice started 'God Save The King'. In a moment the National Anthem was taken up everywhere. It swelled out deep-throatedly.

As the last notes of the Anthem died out, the King stepped down from the verandah. He stood there surrounded by hundreds of men, talking to them, asking them about their experiences.

Then they broke into song again, this time with 'For He's a Jolly Good Fellow'.

May 18th   1891

A Royal daughter

H.R.H. Princess Alexandra rushed to her daughter's bedside in the early hours of the morning and was delighted with her new grandchild. The Duchess of Fife had given birth to a daughter.

When Princess Alexandra wrote to Prince George about the event she related:

"At five o'clock, thank God, I was a happy Grandmother and held my little naked grandchild in my arms! It squeaked like a little sucking-pig!"

May 19th   1536

Queen Anne beheaded

The King fell in love with Anne Boleyn when he was married to Katharine of Aragon.

He persuaded her relentlessly but to his surprise and consternation she refused to become his Mistress.

He wrote her passionate letters which were carried by Royal Messengers to her father's house in Kent. "I promise I shall take you alone for my mistress and put all others out of my thoughts and affections and serve you only."

Anne, sent back a teasing reply.

The King approached Rome for the annulment of his marriage. After six years he was still pleading with Anne who was branded as

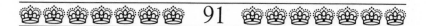

being a Witch in league with the Devil because she could still keep
him at fever-pitch.

Pressed by the King, who was also pressed by Anne in 1533 the
Archbishop of Canterbury defied Rome and declared that Henry
and Katharine had never been husband and wife.

Within a week Anne was crowned Queen. A daughter was born
in 1533 and Christened Elizabeth. Two years later Queen
Katharine died and Henry and Anne celebrated with a huge
banquet.

But as the deposed Queen was buried Anne miscarried. It was the
beginning of the end.

King Henry fell in love with one of her Ladies-in-Waiting and on
the 19th May 1536 Anne was beheaded.

May 20th   1884

Wise advice

Queen Victoria wrote many letters to her granddaughter Victoria
who became on her marriage the Princess Louis of Battenberg.
Following her marriage in April 1884 the Queen wrote:

"Darling Victoria . . . Take care of yourself, dear Child, don't
ride too much and above *all not* if you were not regular in other
respects. It might injure your health for ever.

"Don't mind me saying this – but you know I am so anxious for
your happiness and health and strength and no one else may tell
you,

"Ever your devoted Grandmama
V. R. I."

March 21st 1818

A Happy Marriage. When H.R.H. The Duke of Clarence married Princess Adelaide of Saxe-Meiningen, he was 52, she was 25. The marriage proved an instant, total and lasting success.

March 24th 1603

H.M. Queen Elizabeth dies at Richmond Palace, between the hours of two and three in the morning.

March 25th 1875

H.R.H. The Prince of Wales came to spend a day with the Princesse de Sagan. Her son, aged 15, had developed violent feelings about the affair and seeing His Royal Highness's clothes on a chair, threw them into a fountain.

April 5th 1933

H.M. George V was delighted with Elizabeth his daughter-in-law, and wrote to his son 'Bertie', the Duke of York: 'The better I know and the more I see of your dear little wife, the more charming I think she is and everyone falls in love with her . . .'

April 14th 1630

H.M. Queen Henrietta Maria attended a banquet where she was presented
with a pie. From it leapt a dwarf called Jeffrey Hudson, only 18 inches tall.

May 19th 1536

H.M. King Henry VIII fell in love with Anne Boleyn when married to Katharine of Aragon but the love did not last. King Henry then fell for one of the Queen's Ladies-in-Waiting and Queen Anne was beheaded.

May 21st 1662

Fifteen-year-old Catherine of Braganza became the wife of H.M. King
Charles II. Afterwards he wrote that he was very sleepy on his wedding
night.

May 24th 1839

Queen Victoria wrote in her Journal. 'This day I go out of my TEENS and become 20.' She attended a Ball and found herself falling in love with the Russian Grand Duke.

May 21st   1662

A sleepy bridegroom

H.M. King Charles II, a handsome dashing roué, married fifteen-year-old Catherine of Braganza.

The Queen was shy and gauche and in the years to come she was unable to compete with the sexual attractions of the beautiful rivals for her husband's affections.

King Charles, on first acquaintance, was pleased with Catherine but on the day after their wedding he wrote:

'It was happy for the honour of the Nation that I was not put to the consummation of the marriage last night; for I was so sleepy by having slept but two hours on my journey I was afraid matters would have gone very sleepily.'

May 22nd   1668

The "Blue Terror"

King Louis XIV gave Madame de Montespan a huge diamond known as 'The Blue Terror'. Considered to be one of the most evil stones on earth it was originally the eye of a Hindu Idol and was stolen by robbers.

Madame de Montespan quickly lost her Royal lover. Queen Marie Antoinette suffered after she possessed it.

There were two Royal Families whose possession of the diamond was followed by disasters and deaths.

It is now known as 'The Hope Diamond' but there is no hope for those who wear it!

May 23rd   1846

H.M. Ludwig I is bewitched

After a short love affair with Alexander Dumas, the beautiful Lola Montez left Paris. Dumas said:

"She has an evil eye and is sure to bring bad luck to anyone who closely links his destiny with hers."

On this Autumn morning, H.M. King Ludwig I of Bavaria, 61 years old, was giving audience in his Palace at Munich. A Minister who had recently seen Lola Montez handed the King her formal petition craving an audience.

"She is extremely beautiful Sir," he murmured. Without waiting for permission Lola rushed past the Guards and stood magnificent and challenging before the Monarch.

Nothing more beautiful existed amongst all the Art treasures of Munich than Lola at this moment.

The King looked at her unnerved by such loveliness and his questioning gaze told Lola of his doubts. From her breast she suddenly brought for a stiletto, without which she rarely moved. In one quick stroke she slashed her bodice straight down the centre of her bosom.

Ludwig saw her appearance was as God had made her. The stiletto could not reveal the mind the Devil had added.

"I was bewitched," the King confessed soon afterwards. It was the evil eye which finally cost him his throne.

May 24th   1839

'Grown up'

Queen Victoria wrote in her Journal. "This day I go out of my TEENS and become 20."

As part of the celebrations she attended a Ball at St. George's Hall. The Russian Grand Duke was present and she found herself falling in love with him.

"I really am quite in love with the Grand Duke; he is a dear, delightful young man."

May 25th   1660

A jewel for the King

Before dawn King Charles II was pacing impatiently on the quay of Dover Harbour. His Majesty's beloved sister Minette was arriving from France.

"I can never tell you," he wrote, "too often how touchingly and passionately I love you, my dearest Minette."

Ill-treated by her depraved and vicious husband she had only one great hope that Charles would be successful.

They spent some precious happy weeks together until at last she had to return to France.

The King gave her innumerable presents and she sent for her jewel box and offered him anything in it.

It was brought by a very lovely French girl Louise du Keroualle. The King took her hand saying:

"This is the jewel I wish you would leave me."

May 26th   1867

Just May

The Princess May of Teck was christened by the Archbishop of Canterbury. The names given were Victoria (after her godmother), Mary Augusta Louise Olga Pauline Claudine Agnes.

In the family however she was just known as May after the month in which she was born. She was to become the wife of King George V and although they loved each other deeply they found it impossible to express their feelings in words.

They therefore wrote passionate love letters to each other.

May 27th   1972

Uncle David

During her State visit to France The Queen called on her Uncle the Duke of Windsor who was once King Edward VIII. He was seventy-eight and very ill with cancer.

He was, however, determined to be up to see his niece and the needles and tubes by which he was fed were removed. It took the doctors over four hours to get him ready.

The Queen arrived at his house in the Bois de Boulogne and was received by the Duchess who took her upstairs to the Duke's Sitting-Room.

Her Majesty did most of the talking for the Duke, very exhausted, could hardly speak.

Just over a week later 'Black Diamond' the Duke's favourite pug who always lay at the foot of his bed, lay on the floor, his head turned away.

One of the Doctors remarked:
"See! The dog knows what is happening."
On the 28th May the Duke died peacefully in his sleep.

May 28th   1908

Saved by flowers

Queen Amelia of France saw her husband Charles I and her elder
son assassinated in front of her as they drove in their carriage.

They were shot at point-blank range, but The Queen managed to
save her younger son by quickly throwing her bouquet in the
Assassin's face.

May 29th   1630

A lusty lad

H.M. Queen Henrietta Maria had at last given birth to a
screaming, lusty lad – Charles the 'son of our love'. He was a
solemn baby who slept a lot.

'The nurses told me,' the Venetian ambassador reported, 'that
after his birth he never clenched his fists but always kept his hands
open. From this they augur that he will be a Prince of great
liberality!'

Which he was both as Prince and King.

May 30th   1660

A King's revenge

After the wild jubilation of King Charles II's return and when he
had ridden into London on his thirtieth birthday, he was told of the
grand funeral that had taken place for Oliver Cromwell.

King Charles had the bodies of Cromwell and two other regicides
exhumed, dragged through the streets to Tyburn, hanged, beheaded and their heads stuck up on poles in Westminster Hall.

Their bodies were flung into the common pit at Tyburn.

Cromwell's skull remained rotting on a pole late into the reign of
King James II seventeen years later. It was then blown down in a
violent storm.

May 31st   1906

Danger in Spain

H.M. King George V and Queen Mary attended the controversial wedding of Princess Ena of Battenberg only daughter of Princess
Beatrice and H.M. King Alfonso of Spain.

The news that his Cousin Ena was prepared to change to the
Catholic faith surprised and perturbed King George. Many people
felt that he should not attend the ceremony, but with the Queen he
set off on the tiring rail journey to Madrid.

They were, although not aware of it, facing the most dramatic
moment of their lives. But for a coincidence and a stroke of luck
they would have been blown to pieces.

King Alfonso had been warned that an Anarchist was on the
prowl and, when the Bride's procession arrived he thought his fears
were groundless.

However, on the way back the assassin struck. By the mercy of
God, none of the Royal guests was injured.

JUNE

June 1st   1814

The Regent, the world's most famous diamond

Today Napoleon Bonaparte was crowned Emperor of France. Having started life as a Corsican corporal, it pleased him to wear in the hilt of his sword, the most famous diamond in the world.

The Regent Diamond was in the 18th century found by a slave in India. It was stolen from him by the British Captain of a ship and sold in Bombay for 2000 dollars. Obtained by William Pitt, Governor of Madras, it was then sold to the Duke of Orleans, Regent of France, for two and a half million pounds.

In 1814 the Empress Marie Louise escaped from Paris with the Crown Jewels. She was in constant danger of being stopped and searched.

When the Second Empire fell in 1870 the Commune gleefully demanded the jewels but they had been hidden in a ship.

The Commune was crushed in May 1871 and the Regent, the World's most famous diamond, went back to the Louvre.

June 2nd   1953

A Queen in the rain

At the Coronation of H.M. Queen Elizabeth II, no one who saw Queen Salote in person or on television will ever forget the sight.

Six feet tall and weighing nineteen stones, she came from the Commonwealth Kingdom of Tonga.

Despite the pouring rain she sat bolt upright in her landau, waving and blowing kisses and beaming at the crowds, refusing to put up either hood or umbrella.

She endeared herself to everybody who saw her.

June 3rd   1227

A Royal Saint

Queen Elizabeth of Hungary, wife of King Louis IV, Landgraf of Thuringia, was turned out of her Castle by her brother-in-law when it was learnt that the King had died whilst on a Crusade.

She had already astonished the Court by her piety and good works. Now she put on a Nun's robe and moved to a tiny cottage at the foot the the hill below the Castle.

She devoted herself to caring for the sick and poor, spending all the money she owned on them.

She died worn out and prematurely aged, although she was only twenty-four, and was canonised four years later.

June 4th   1761

So brief a love

At a Ball held to celebrate his birthday in 1761, King George III, knowing that he would soon be pledged to a Princess he had never

met, allowed himself reckless dalliance with the famous beauty Lady Sarah Lennox.

The guests, glancing with constant curiosity towards the throne, saw the King looking handsome and eager and, it appeared to Fox, 'displaying the strongest symptoms of love and desire.'

During the following weeks Lady Sarah dressed up every morning as a country girl and pretended to make hay in a field near Holland House, past which the King was accustomed to ride. She looked bewitching.

However, in early July she learned of the King's proposed marriage and was justifiably angry, calling him a hypocrite in a letter to her best friend Lady Susan Fox-Strangeways.

Yet she had forgiven him almost before the ink was dry on the paper, and was more worried about her pet squirrel which was sick than His Majesty.

She was pleased to know she would be a bridesmaid at the wedding.

June 5th   1938

The Crown of King Charlemagne

When Hitler annexed Austria he demanded that the crown of King Charlemagne be brought to Neurenberg.

This crown of gold, enamel, pearls and precious stones, is the most venerable of all the crowns in the world, and was used by King Charlemagne.

It was made for Otto I the founder of the Holy Roman Empire of Germany and was modelled by Otto III who added extra gems.

The Austrian Curator tried to defend the crown by pointing out that it carried enamelled portraits of two Jews, David and Solomon. Hitler hesitated, but pressed his demand nevertheless.

When the Americans liberated Neurenberg they had a great deal of trouble in finding the crown.

Under pressure the Mayor admitted that Hitler had hidden it. The Americans climbed down into The Bunker deep underground where they found sealed inside a wall the locked copper chest containing the crown of Charlemagne.

It was returned to Austria where it remains to this day.

June 6th   1922

An insular King

H.M. Queen Mary went abroad three times between 1922 and 1925 and after that never left the shores of Britain.

It was not that she did not want to go: it was simply that her husband King George V hated foreign travel.

His view was:

"Amsterdam, Rotterdam and all the other dams. Damned if I'll go!"

June 7th   1394

Grief for a Queen

Richard II's wife, Queen Anne, died at Sheen in Surrey, which
was the King's favourite Palace.

It was one of the select group of Royal residences in the Thames
Valley favoured by Edward III (he died there on June 21st in 1377).

Richard II had improved the Palace and built one of the first
Summer Houses on an adjoining island.

Yet upon the Queen's death he ordered the Palace to be
destroyed and the site left desolate.

June 8th   1851

Brave love

On the fourth anniversary of the wedding of H.R.H. Prince
George Duke of Cambridge he wrote to his wife:

"You alone know love, or ought to know, how blessed and happy
I feel that this day made you my own and me yours."

They had met on the same day as Queen Victoria's Wedding, the
10th February 1840.

A Cousin of the Queen, Prince George, had been abroad for
some time to avoid being forced, it was whispered, into marriage
with his Cousin Victoria.

Prince George had already announced that arranged marriages
were doomed to failure and he was determined not to marry anyone
he did not love.

Louisa Fairbrother was an actress and her father was a partner in a printing firm in Bow Street where she lived.

She had acted on the stage at Drury Lane, the Lyceum and Covent Garden.

She had a classical beauty and elegance, and was a graceful dancer.

Her compelling charm however, did not prevent Prince George's family from being horrified at the marriage.

The Prince's wife was called Mrs. FitzGeorge and had three children.

Their life was summed up later – 'he had a fine woman, he married her and stuck to her.'

June 9th   1939

The Queen – victorious

H.M. Queen Elizabeth, wife of King George VI gained the headlines of *'THE BRITISH RE-TAKE WASHINGTON'*

The fairytale sight of her in crinoline ball-gown and tiara captivated not only the public, but also the professional onlookers when she and the King visited America.

At a time when the Americans were insisting that the evils of Hitler and his jackal Mussolini were of no concern 'to us over here', they did much to re-build Anglo-American understanding. Her Majesty was nominated 'Woman of the Year'.

June 10th   1882

The Prince and Princess of Wales plant an oak tree

In the newly opened Abbey Park in Leicester their Royal
Highnesses were received with the pomp and lavishness usual on
such occasions.

The 'Illustrated London News' reported on June 10th:

'There was but one incident of a slightly disagreeable character: a
tipsy fellow thrust himself close up to the carriage of their Royal
Highnesses, and insisted upon asking the Princess to shake hands
with him. He was instantly hustled away, and consigned to the
police.

The next day he was brought before the Mayor and Magistrates:
they inflicted a sentence of twenty-one days imprisonment. But
when the Prince and Princess read of this in the Daily Newspaper
they telegraphed to the Mayor, begging that the foolish man should
be forgiven.

Accordingly he was released.'

June 11th   1903

The "Black Prophecy" comes true

H.M. King Alexander I of Serbia was awkward and ungainly. He
wore pince-nez and with his receding hair, he looked more like a
middle-aged member of the Intelligentsia rather than a young King
in his twenties.

He insisted on marrying a fascinating Serbian widow a few years older than himself, Donna Draga Mashin. It made him exceedingly unpopular.

There was a conspiracy hatched among the Army officers to overthrow him. King Alexander soon realised that his throne and probably his life were in danger. He made himself ill with worry, suffering with insomnia and brooding over the 'Black Prophecy' of a peasant who foretold the extinction of the Obrenovics.

The 'Black Prophecy' came true on the hot and sultry night on 10th June 1903. Troops surrounded the Palace in Belgrade and a party of officers forced their way in searching for the King and Queen.

Finding them hidden in a secret chamber off their bedroom, they shot them down, and slashed them with their swords.

June 12th   1727

A sad ending

When George Augustus Prince of Wales was told by Walpole who had had the news earlier, that he was King George II he exclaimed:

"Dat is one big lie."

But as the King he was to remain steady on his Throne throughout the invasion of The Young Pretender who came within 150 miles of London and his words with which he had cheered his troops to victory were always remembered:

"Now for the honour of England! Fire and be brave. ."

Yet as a brave soldier and a brave King he had an ignominious death.

He suffered from constipation and he strained his heart fatally when attempting to move his bowels.

June 13th   1930

A Fairy makes the Princess laugh

H.R.H. The Princess Elizabeth attended a party at Londonderry House given by Lady Plunket, a great friend of her Mother's.

She was four and a half years of age and the children at the party were all in Fancy dress. The Princess saw a Fairy held in the arms of her Nanny and danced up to it.

"What a pretty baby," she said. "What is her name?"

"Raine, Your Royal Highness," Nanny replied.

The Princess went into a peal of laughter.

"What a funny, funny name!" she exclaimed.

The baby was to become The Countess Spencer, Step-Mother of H.R.H. Princess Diana, The Princess of Wales.

June 14th   1833

King William IV at Royal Ascot Races

The weather was charming, the Course crowded, and the King was received pleasantly.

His household at Windsor Castle was so ill managed that his grooms were drunk every day while one man who *was* sober, was killed going home from the Races.

It is said that no-one exercised any authority and in consequence the household all ran riot.

June 15th   1330

A hero is born

A son is born to H.M. King Edward III and Philippa of Hainault, at Woodstock, who twenty-one years later was to marry Countess Joan, 'The Fair Maid of Kent' with whom he was wildly in love.

Known as 'The Black Prince' because of the colour of his armour, he became a romantic hero, famous in tournaments as well as in battle. He was closely associated with the establishment of the Order of the Garter.

He was 'the flower of chivalry of all the world!'

June 16th   1878

The King's broken heart

H. C. M. King Alfonso XII of Spain was only nineteen when he announced that he intended to marry Mercedes, the sixteen-year-old daughter of the Duke de Montpensier. They had been in love for two years.

His mother 'was outraged'. She had already decided that her son should marry the Pretender's eldest daughter Blanca, who was only ten at the time.

Alfonso however said:

"I will never marry against my will."

Mercedes was beautiful, delicate and distinguished, with 'huge dark eyes shadowed with sweeping lashes, and her hair was the true Andalusian black.'

The engagement was celebrated in December 1877 and a month later they were married with great pomp, with music, dancing and Royal Bull Fights.

They were so happy they radiated their love to everyone around them. Yet five months after their marriage Mercedes died of gastric fever. The King's grief was heart-breaking. He never really recovered.

The young and happy part of him had gone.

June 17th   1866

A very strange dejeuner

The vulgarity as well as the extravagance of the Courtesans of the Second Empire was unsurpassed in any other period.

Madame Musard was one of the most beautiful and had an infatuated lover in the King of the Netherlands.

A Journalist wrote on this day:

'A curious *dejeuner* was given yesterday by Madame Musard. Her enormous fortune of one million pounds sterling, her beauty, her seat on horseback, horses, carriages, '*hotels*', stables and the rest are things that have been talked about and displayed.'

The guests assembled in a long Gallery draped with green curtains. Breakfast was served and eaten, coffee and cigars followed.

Then a bell rang and all the draperies were were suddenly withdrawn, and where did the guests find themselves? Why, in a stables, where stood eighteen magnificent horses which had also breakfasted but not off truffles, champagne and cigars behind the curtains.

June 18th   1837

The Battle of Waterloo

H.M. William IV was ill, but the bulletins were issued only a few days before his death. Then they were displayed in St. James's Palace to which the Nobility were admitted. An order for him to be prayed for in Churches was issued on Friday 6th June.

The King realised it was Waterloo Day on the 18th.

"Doctor, I know that I am going," he had said a few days previously, "but I would like to see another Anniversary. Try to see if you cannot tinker me up to last out that day."

His Majesty got his wish. He did last out and lay clasping a Tricolour captured at the Battle. He also insisted that the Annual Waterloo Dinner at the Castle should take place as usual.

June 19th   1972

Love at first sight

H.M. King Carl XVI Gustaf of Sweden attended the Olympics in Munich and said later:

"Something went 'click' in my mind, and it was love at first sight."

The young King was attending the Munich Olympics in 1972 when he met Silvia Sommerlath who was acting as principal hostess to visiting V.I.P.s.

King Carl was a keen yachtsman, a skilled scuba diver, and a water-skier. He was also a cross-country skier, and fencing and swimming were among his other sports.

He was also interested in technical research and material science.

Silvia had specialised in languages and graduated at the University of Dusseldorf.

The marriage was to take place in Stockholm in July 1976, and the Wedding Breakfast at the Castle included Scottish wood-pigeon.

After the Ceremony at the Cathedral, the Bride and Bridegroom sailed in a Royal Barge to the Royal Palace, and a crowd of 180,000 lined the streets and more than five million watched on television.

June 20th   1837

H.R.H. The Princess Victoria becomes Queen

At twelve minutes past two on this morning the young Victoria lay asleep in her mother's bedroom.

The Archbishop of Canterbury accompanied by the Lord Chamberlain, Lord Conyingham and the King's Physician, travelled straight from the Royal deathbed to Kensington Palace.

When they arrived it was about 5 a.m. It took some time to persuade the Duchess of Kent to awaken Princess Victoria.

At six o'clock the Duchess, carrying a silver candlestick came into the room with her daughter.

The Princess was wearing a cotton dressing gown over her nightgown and her long fair hair streamed down her back.

As she entered she saw her visitors fall on their knees and heard Lord Conyingham's explanatory phrases.

When he reached the word "Queen" she held out her hand for him to kiss and said:

"I will be good."

June 21st   1547

The heart of a King

At his Coronation H.M. King Henri of France was determined that the whole of France and everyone else in the world should know of his devotion to his mistress, Diane de Poitiers.

She was eighteen years older than he was but he was madly in love and on a glorious June day he appeared under a triumphal arch bearing the monogram 'H D' embroidered on his tunic with pearls and jewels.

The same letters were on the liveries of the personal guard who wore Diane's colours of black and white.

Diane de Poitiers was the most beautiful woman anyone had ever seen and their love affair lasted for nearly a quarter of a century and became legendary throughout Europe.

She virtually ruled the Kingdom but with a brilliance that made it one of the most remarkable reigns in French history typified by a national and international policy which was wise, just and far-seeing.

June 22nd   1910

A practical joke

At the Coronation of King George V and Queen Mary among the guests was H.C.H. Crown Prince William of Germany, eldest son of the Kaiser and soon to be known in fighting Britain as 'Little Willy'. He was an honoured guest and staying at Buckingham Palace.

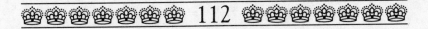

The Crown Prince was fond of practical jokes. To keep up strength during the hours to be spent in Westminster Abbey, he took along with him a bottle of brandy.

He was seated next to the Crown Prince of Turkey, a Mohammedan and not supposed to drink alcohol. Prince William took a swig and, out of mischief, passed the bottle to his neighbour.

To his delight, the Turk took a long, strong pull and thanked the donor profusely.

June 23rd   1910

The 20th Prince of Wales

H.M. George V created his son David the Prince of Wales on 23 June and, before the Coronation, invested him with the Order of the Garter.

At the instigation of Mr David Lloyd George, an old custom was revived: it was planned that, at a ceremony at Caernarvon Castle, Prince David would be presented to the people of the Principality of Wales. The ceremony was planned for July 1911.

When Prince David learned what he had to wear, he objected, and there followed a blazing row with his father at Windsor, a row which was calmed down by his mother, Queen Mary. In his own words:

"When a tailor appeared to measure me for a fantastic costume designed for the occasion, consisting of white satin breeches and a mantle and surcoat of purple velvet edged with ermine, I decided that things had gone too far . . . . . what would my Navy friends say if they saw me in this preposterous rig?"

"There was a family blow-up that night: but in the end my Mother, as always, smoothed things over.

"You mustn't take a mere ceremony so seriously," she said.

June 24th   1791

A disastrous muddle

At Easter 1791, H.M. Louis XVI wanted to go to St-Cloud to take Communion from the hands of a non-oath-swearing Priest.

The mob refused to let him leave the Tuileries, and he then had the idea of putting into operation the plan for his flight thought out by Mirabeau and organised by Count Fersen.

During the night of 20–21 June 1791, Louis XVI, disguised as a lackey, Queen Marie-Antoinette, provided with a Danish passport, the Dauphin, dressed as a girl, Madame Elizabeth, the King's sister, and Madame Royale managed to leave the Tuileries in secret.

A too ostentatious coach took them in the direction of Montmedy. At the same time the Count of Provence had taken the road to Brussels and reached there without any impediment.

On the morning of the 21 June, Paris was astounded to hear the news of the King's flight. To avoid worrying consequences of it La Fayette announced that the King had been kidnapped and sent his messengers after him with a warrant for his arrest.

Because of unwise moves, the King had been recognised on the road. A postmaster called Drouet caught up with him and made the coach stop at Varennes-en-Argonne, where La Fayette's emissary, Romeuf, arrived just in time to make the arrest.

The Royal family had to return to Paris and to death.

June 25th   1807

Alexander I sues for an Armistice

To the amazement of the Russian people the Emperor decided to sue for an Armistice with France. He met Napoleon on a sumptuously appointed raft in the middle of the Niemen.

The Russian Officers who accompanied him were instructed 'to be civil to the French', to remember Napoleon's imperial title and not to refer to him as 'Bonaparte'.

The Regimental Chaplains, however, carried in their pockets copies of the Synod proclamation denouncing Bonaparte as 'the Servant of Satan and the worshipper of whores and idols'.

June 26th   1830

Death of King George IV

Raffish, pleasure seeking, flamboyant, hopelessly extravagant, but the First Gentleman in Europe with an unerring judgement of Art which was not appreciatred during his life time, King George IV was always attracted by women older than himself.

His secret marriage to Mrs. Maria FitzHerbert was never revealed and she passed completely out of his life before he became Regent.

Yet when he died a black ribbon round his neck revealed a diamond locket containing the miniature portrait of Mrs. Fitzherbert.

He had always believed she was his true wife.

June 27th   1868

Leaving Russia with a Grand Duke

Caroline Letessier spent a fortune which did *not* come from the *Theatre du Palais-Royal* where she was an actress from 1855–1856.

Her elegance, her beauty and her blithe disregard for money made her a Prince's Mistress.

In 1859 she went to St. Petersburg where she stayed for eight years and ensnared a Grand Duke.

Her behaviour, however, caused the Russian Authorities to insist on her departure.

On this day she set off from Russia with her Grand Duke and they travelled as *Monsieur et Madame* Letessier.

At Berlin the Chief of Police came to demand their passports.

"Are you looking for me?" enquired His Imperial Highness.

"Yes, *Monseigneur*, we want Your Imperial Highness to go back to St. Petersburg."

"But I don't choose to return to Russia. *Madame* is going to France, and I'm going with her."

"I am sorry, *Monseigneur*. Your uncle, the Emperor's orders."

"You wouldn't dare to arrest me?"

"No, *Monseigneur*, but we shall detach the compartment from the train, so you won't go. As for *Madame*, she can set off if she likes."

June 28th   1838

H.M. Queen Victoria is crowned

The congregation was deeply moved by the poignant dignity of the child-like figure in the centre of the nave of Westminster Abbey.

A ray of sunshine fell on her head as she was crowned Queen of England by the Archbishop of Canterbury. All the Peers and Peeresses put on their coronets, the silver trumpets sounded and the Archbishop presented The Queen to the people turning her to the East, West, North and South.

During the Ceremony the Archbishop crushed the ruby ring on her fourth finger not noticing that it had inadvertently been made to fit the fifth. The Queen got it off again with great pain and only after bathing it in iced water.

The Archbishop tried to give her the Orb after she had already got it.

During the Homage Lord Rolle, nearly ninety, caught his foot in his robes on the steps of the throne and rolled to the bottom. As he struggled to his feet and tried again to make the perilous ascent, cheering broke out.

It became a tornado when the Queen anxiously whispering "May I not get up and meet him?" saved him the risk of another fall.

At the end of five hours Queen Victoria drove home in State. Someone considered she looked "white and tremulous" and murmured:

"Poor little Queen, she is at an age at which a girl can hardly be trusted to choose a bonnet for herself, yet a task is laid upon her from which an Archangel might shrink."

Inside Buckingham Palace the Queen had one more duty to perform. She gathered up her skirts and ran up to her room to give her dog Dash his bath.

June 29th   1828

No jokes from the Jockey Club

King George IV dined at St. James's Palace for the Jockey Club Dinner where all the guests were men.

They assembled in the Throne Room where His Majesty was waiting for them, looking very well and walking about. He soon however, sat down and asked everyone else to do the same.

Nobody spoke, and he laughed and said:

"This is more like a Quaker than a Jockey Club Meeting."

June 30th   1688

An invitation to invade

H.R.H. William Prince of Orange received today an invitation to invade England. It was signed by a representative selection of King James II's opponents.

Prince William landed at Tor Bay in Devon in November and proceeded almost unopposed to London.

The following April, William and his wife Mary, were crowned King and Queen.

JULY

July 1st   1830

The King economizes

Shocked by the extravagances of his late brother H.M. King George IV, as soon as he came to the throne H.M. King William started on this day to economise.

The number of Royal Yachts was cut down from five to two. The German Band was dismissed and replaced by a less skilful and much cheaper substitute. He sacked the French Chefs who had previously followed the King from Residence to Residence.

This piece of frugality was deplored by many of those who ate habitually at the Royal table. 'Detestable', Phillip van Neumann wrote of the Royal cuisine.

Lord Dudley who was famous for his *sotto voce* remarks grumbled: "What a change to be sure – cold pâté and hot champagne."

July 2nd   1925

Une femme fatale

H.R.H. King Carol of Roumania had an emotional hunger for love and understanding.

Tall, handsome and extremely intelligent everyone expected he would be a popular and successful monarch. He was however, fatally weak where women were concerned.

He made a run-away marriage in 1918 which was annulled, he fell in love with the beautiful Princess Helen of Greece and married her.

But in 1925 he met Elena Lupescu. She forced Carol to renounce his rights to the Throne.

When his father died and the Government invited him to return as Roumania's King Elena followed him. He promised she would stay away but her influence caused him to be rude to his mother and unkind to his wife.

When in 1940 Hitler engineered his deposition and forced him into exile Carol had no friends left.

Elena never lost her passionate allure for him. When they were in Portugal they were married in a Civil Ceremony in 1947 and a religious one in 1949.

July 3rd   1423

A King saved miraculously

H.M. King Charles VII of France and Mary of Anjou gave birth to a son who was to become Louis XI of France.

Just after the birth while King Charles was at a meeting at La Rochelle, the floor collapsed. Though His Majesty was miraculously unhurt, many people were killed, and the catastrophe worsened his hypochondria.

July 4th   1939

First meeting

H.R.H. Princess Elizabeth celebrated her 13th birthday and began, significantly, to study British history more seriously for the first time under the Vice-Provost of Eton College, Sir Henry Marten. It was to be the last year of peace for six years.

On a visit to Dartmouth in July she was introduced to Lord Mountbatten's nephew, an 18-year old naval cadet, Prince Philip of Greece.

The Prince devoured a large plateful of shrimps as the Princess watched, wide-eyed and speechless.

July 5th   1816

A sad end

The actress Mrs. Dorothy Jordan, H.R.H. The Duke of Clarence's mistress for twenty years who had borne him ten children, died in France.

Abandoned, almost destitute, she had nothing left to live for.

All his life King William spoke of her with great affection. Whenever a portrait of Mrs. Jordan came on the market he would buy it and add it to his collection.

When he became King he commissioned a bust of Mrs. Jordan from the sculptor Chantrey and announced that it was destined for St. Paul's.

To his annoyance the Chapter politely refused the proffered honour and the bust remained under the tolerant eye of Queen Adelaide.

Around it clustered other relics of his raffish past which the King never forgot.

July 6th   1662

One law for the man

H.M. King Charles II never allowed his courtiers to behave disrespectfully towards his wife, Queen Catherine.

One day she asked him:

"What do you English mean, when you squeeze a lady by the hand?"

The King replied that he would tell her if she told him whose conduct had made her ask the question. She said it was Edward Montague, her Master of the Horse, who had squeezed her hand whenever he helped her into her coach.

Montague was sent from Windsor, never to return.

The Queen however became resigned to the King's selfishness and constant unfaithfulness. Once when she went to his bedroom and noticed a tiny slipper protruding from behind a curtain, she laughed and withdrew quickly.

"Lest," she said, "the pretty little fool, whoever it is, hiding behind the curtain, should catch cold."

July 7th   1789

All at sea

H.R.H. King George III's Court moves to Weymouth accompanied by Queen Charlotte's two favourite dogs, Badine and Phillis. The latter is a very small, very timid, very beautiful Italian greyhound which had previously belonged to Frederick the Great.

During the visit the King went for a dip in the sea. Miss Burney recorded:

"The King bathes, and with great success; a machine follows the Royal one into the sea, filled with fiddlers, who play '*God Save The King*', as His Majesty takes the plunge!"

July 8th   1938

The Countess of Strathmore dies

The Countess was charming, sympathetic and understanding to everyone she met as well as to her family. She also had an amusing wit and once said:

"Some people have to be fed Royalty like sea-lions with fish".

Her daughter, Her Majesty the Queen was bereaved ten days before a State Visit to Paris which had been planned for a long time. Everyone was in despair at the thought of her being received by the best-dressed and most *chic* nation in the world entirely in gloomy black.

However Her Majesty's Couturier Norman Hartnell, remembered that black was not the only colour of mourning.

By working day and night he was able to turn despair into triumph by dressing the Queen entirely in white.

She looked dazzlingly beautiful and overwhelmed all Paris into an effusive and very sincere expression of admiration.

July 9th   1946

The King mystified

H.M. King George VI, an expert on Military decorations, noticed one day at Windsor that Lord Gowrie was wearing on his tunic both the China Medal for the Relief of the Peking Legations as well as Queen Victoria's Medal for the first part of the South African War.

He asked somebody later:

"Have you ever known a case of another man holding *both* those medals? I never have! How on earth did he get from China to South Africa in time?"

July 10th   1947

A popular engagement

The engagement between H.R.H. Princess Elizabeth and Lieutenant Philip Mountbatten, R. N. is announced.

The young and very happy couple immediately drove to Marlborough House and received congratulations from Queen Mary, they then attended a Royal garden party at Buckingham Palace.

At 9.20 pm they appeared on the Centre Balcony and were cheered by a huge crowd.

The whole country was thrilled by the news – Princess Elizabeth had captured the heart of the Nation.

July 11th   1896

The drawn sword

Today Queen Victoria held a garden party at Buckingham Palace.

There were 5,000 guests assembled on a brilliant hot and sunny day.

As they roamed over the beautifully kept green lawns beside the lake they presented a dazzling sight in their coloured uniforms, picture hats, and long floating muslin dresses.

In the centre was the Queen, sitting in her carriage drawn by two grey horses, and behind her came her family; the Prince of Wales, the Duke and Duchess of York, the old Duke of Cambridge and Princess Beatrice with Princess Ena.

The Queen's customary black accoutrements were relieved by white feathers and a rose in her bonnet. There were pearls round her neck and she carried a white parasol.

At one of the last garden parties given by the Queen it was so hot in the Royal tea tent that one of the ladies fainted.

A quick-thinking Guards officer drew his sword and grandly cut a hole in the tent to let in some air.

His weapon pierced the backside of an unfortunate waitress standing without.

July 12th   1223

A Prince is lost

H.M. King Philip Augustus of France prepared to secure the throne for his young son[*] by crowning him before he died. The Prince's accession was accompanied by a rather strange incident.

One day Philip Augustus gave his son permission to go hunting. The party was soon in the forest, chasing a wild boar.

The Prince, who was riding a swift horse, soon found himself lost, and as the night set in he became seriously alarmed.

After having wandered about for several hours he saw a light which turned out to be a peasant who was blowing the fire of a charcoal kiln.

The Prince told him who he was and what had happened but he was still considerably afraid. The peasant was a large rough-looking man holding an enormous axe and appearing even more ferocious by being blackened with charcoal dust.

His behaviour, however, did not accord with his appearance for he immediately returned the Prince to his father.

But fear and fatigue threw the boy into a violent fever and the Coronation had to be postponed.

[*]the future Louis VIII (the Lion)

July 13th   1866

For ever and ever

Tzar Alexander II of Russia was a tired, lonely, disillusioned sensual man of forty-two.

He saw Catherine when she was twelve years old and lost his heart.

The Tzar began to court her with bon-bons and flowers until in the Imperial Pavilion in the park of the Winter Palace Catherine became his mistress.

After that every day he managed to snatch an hour or two with her, and he became her slave, her adorer, "his life. . his idol. . for ever."

Their first child was born secretly in 1872 in the Tzar's Study, and there were more children in the following years.

In June 1880 the unhappy Tzarina died.

Forty days later the Tzar married his adored Catherine with only two witnesses present.

She became Her Serene Highness the Princess Yurievsky – her children taking the same name.

July 14th   1917

The family of Windsor

During the war of 1914–1918 there was a lot of comment about the Royal Family having a German name.

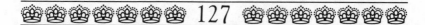

H.M. King George V in response to H. G. Wells's denouncement of 'an alien and uninspiring Court', exclaimed:

"I may be uninspiring but I'll be damned if I'm, an alien!"

The Royal House of Great Britain on this day changed its name from Hanover to Windsor.

Prince Louis of Battenburg took the surname of Mountbatten.

July 15th   1685

A love-child dies

The Duke of Monmouth, the love-son of King Charles II, 'turbulent and irresponsible' handsome and charming is executed at Tower Hill.

He had attempted on this day to wrest the throne from his uncle King James II.

It is believed by a large number of people that a secret marriage had taken place between King Charles II and his first mistress Lucy Walter.

She was described as 'sexy, earthy, arousing, the kind of woman who knows her assets and how best to exploit them'.

King Charles took formal steps to declare there was no truth in this rumour.

Nevertheless, the love the King had for their handsome son, kept the idea alive in the Duke of Monmouth's heart.

July 16th   1654

A Queen forsakes the Throne

On this day at the age of twenty-eight Christina Queen of Sweden renounced the throne and rode away from the Palace as a private person.

She dressed as a man. She went to Flanders, became a Catholic and set out for Rome. Her life after this was one of wild extravagance, frustration and ultimate despair.

Her reign was soon forgotten.

But her abdication when she deliberately threw away her power, was the first incident in a series of events which shaped the boundaries of Eastern Europe and gave the basic pattern of the Russia that emerged under Peter the Great.

July 17th   1429

H.M. King Charles VII of France is crowned

At Rheims Cathedral Joan of Arc stood at the King's side carrying her banner which bore the words 'Jhesus Maria'.

The shepherdess from Lorraine had accomplished her mission – she had won back for France its rightful territory.

Five months earlier she had said to Prince Charles:

"Gentle Dauphin, I tell you on behalf of God my Master that you are the true heir to the throne of France."

July 18th   1833

Aboard the 'Victory'

H.R.H. Princess Victoria visits Portsmouth and Admiral Nelson's flag-ship 'Victory'.

Her Royal Highness wrote in her diary:

"We there received the salute on board. We saw the spot where Nelson fell, and which is covered with a brazen plate and his motto is inscribed on it, 'Every Englishman is expected to do his duty.'

"We went down as low as the tanks, and there tasted the water which had been in there for two years, and which was excellent."

"We also saw the cabin where the Admiral died. We tasted some of the men's beef and potatoes, and likewise drank some grog."

July 19th   1821

Pomp and prejudice

H.M. King George IV is crowned on this day at Westminster Abbey.

He wore a black hat with white ostrich plumes and a 27-foot crimson train covered with gold stars.

The procession was headed for the last time by the King's Herb-Woman. She was followed by the Chief Officers of State, three Bishops and the Peers in order of rank.

As the King entered the Abbey, the Hallelujah Chorus was sung. After a lengthy ceremony the Royal Family and 312 men banqueted in Westminster Hall.

The menu included braised capons, hot joints, lobster, crayfish and cold roast fowl.

However decorum did not triumph – there was the scandal of Queen Caroline attempting hysterically to storm the locked doors and a near riot in Westminster Abbey.

July 20th   1785

Body and soul

On this day there was wild rejoicing on the birth of a son to the Sultan's favourite 'The Beautiful One'.

On her way home to Martinique from her Convent School in Nantes, Aimee Dubuoq was captured by Algerian corsairs.

She was sent by them to Constantinople as a present from the Dey of Algiers to his master Sultan Abd Ul Hamid of Turkey, Allah's Shadow upon Earth.

She entered the Harem and was educated in the seductive arts of love. But Aimee, who was known as Naksh, 'the Beautiful One' had a shrewd little French mind.

It told her that the only possibility for her future was in some way to attract the Sultan not only with her body but with her brain.

The Sultan was a cultured voluptuary with a charm Aimee had not expected. He found her fascinating and she became his favourite.

On the 20th July 1785 her son Mahmoud was born and after that every year Aimee became more powerful.

Secretly she converted the Sultan to Catholicism and even more secretly she married him according to the Rites of the Catholic Church.

After that the Sultan treated her as his wife, consulting her on the policy of the Ottoman Empire until she was in a position to alter and direct it.

July 21st   1859

A tearful Royal farewell

On this day Grand Duke Leopoldo of Tuscany was driven out of his Grand Duchy on the pretext that he refused to go to war with his cousin the Emperor of Austria.

The Florentines stood calmly in the streets to watch their Grand Duke go. He and his family were heartbroken at having to leave and when they reached the heights of Fiesole, the Grand Duke ordered the carriages to stop.

They had a last look at their home and one by one they broke down and wept.

Finally sitting in a teaful row by the roadside they tried to compose themselves, only to find that not one of them had a handkerchief.

The tears coursing down their cheeks already covered with dust, left dirty channels which did not improve the appearance of the Ducal family.

However, the Grand Duchess saved the situation by lifting her skirts, and wiping everyone's tears away with the corner of her petticoat.

July 22nd   1880

An Incident in Paris

H.M. King Edward VII was a great eater and he particularly enjoyed rich food. One night, before he became King, he dined at the Café de Paris in Paris.

The Chef had created a new pancake sauce consisting of maraschino, curacao and kirschwasser which unexpectedly ignited in the pan.

The King amazed and dismayed the Chef by insisting on finishing all the pancakes and named the dish 'Crepes Suzette' as a tribute to his very lovely companion.

July 23rd   1923

Victim of the Revolution

Princess Catherine Yourievsky, daughter of Tzar Alexander II of Russia, makes her debut as a music-hall singer.

She sang a verse from 'Down in the Forest' at the Coliseum Theatre in London.

"I am delighted by my reception," she said. "Singing has become my sole means of maintenance."

July 24th   1886–1925

A strange test

H.R.H. Maharajah of Gwalior was a great admirer of Queen Victoria. He ordered a chandelier to be made identical to the vast one at Buckingham Palace, but larger.

While it was being constructed in Venice he began to doubt if his ceiling could cope with the weight of the chandelier. He decided to try a test.

He strapped up the heaviest of his elephants and had it lifted by crane on to the roof.

Fortunately it did not collapse and the chandelier was installed.

July 25th   1865

A choice

H.M. Otto I of Greece was deposed by his people.

He had had a tempestuous love affair with the entrancing Englishwoman Jane Digby and had not endeared himself to his subjects.

The Greeks offered the throne to Lord Stanley, an English aristocrat who would one day be the fabulously wealthy Earl of Derby, with huge estates in Lancashire.

Lord Stanley turned down the invitation saying he preferred to be the Earl of Derby rather than the King of Greece.

When the Prime Minister Disraeli who had appointed Lord Stanley Secretary of State for Foreign Affairs heard this he said:

"Had I his youth I would not hesitate. Even with the Earldom of Derby in distance it is a dazzling adventure for the House of Stanley, but they are not an adventurous race, and I fancy they would prefer Knowsley to the Parthenon and Lancashire to the Attic Plains."

July 26th   1924

Darby Daisy

The Dowager Countess of Warwick, the beautiful Daisy with whom the late King Edward VII was wildly in love, opened her stately home, Easton Lodge in Essex, for the use of the Labour Party.

Members of Parliament and Trade-union leaders were installed in gilt arm chairs and egg-and-spoon races were run on the green lawns.

Many visitors were perplexed to find photographs of the late King in their bed-rooms.

Occasionally, their hostess pointed out the bed in which The King had slept with her.

July 27th   1944

The Queen inspects the Home Guard

Colonel the Honourable Michael Bowes-Lyon was in command of a battalion of the Home Guard in Bedfordshire. His sister the Queen came to stay with him and inspected his men.

The Colonel had in World War I been a prisoner of the Germans for nearly four years. Soon after his Regiment reached France he was reported as a casualty.

But being possessed with the Bowes-Lyon 'Giftie' or 'Second Sight', his younger brother David refused to wear a black tie.

He said he knew his brother Michael was still alive. He had twice 'seen' him very ill in a large house surrounded by fir trees.

Three months later David Bowes-Lyon was proved right when the family learnt that Michael had been wounded, taken prisoner and was being nursed in a big house surrounded by fir trees.

July 28th   1540

Found guilty

Thomas Cromwell Earl of Essex was beheaded this day. He was actively instrumental in promoting Henry VIII's marriage with Anne of Cleves.

The King, disappointed in his wife, wreaked his vengeance upon his Minister. After the mere shadow of a trial, the Earl was found guilty of high treason and beheaded.

The Earl experienced the same fate as most of the King's confidential Ministers who were overloaded with favours so long as they pleased their Monarch

But the first loss of confidence was a step to the scaffold!

July 29th   1642

Bells for a birth

The bells in the Churches in Lichtenstein were pealing this morning, as the people came out of their houses to go to work.

They looked at each other and the men laughed while the women were half envious, half sympathetic.

The bells were ringing because H.R.H. Prince Hartmann III of Lichtenstein and his wife Elizabeth had another child.

They were to be proved the most prolific Royal couple in the world, producing twenty-four children, twenty-one of whom were born alive.

July 30th   1847

The first dip for a Queen

Queen Victoria first used her Bathing Machine to-day and it is still to be seen at Osborne House.

She recorded the event in her diary:

"Drove down to the beach with my maids and went into the bathing machine, where I undressed and bathed in the sea (for the first time in my life) a very nice bathing woman attending me.

"I thought it delightful till I put my head under the water, when I thought I should be stifled. After dressing again, drove back."

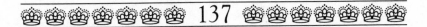

July 31st

A bridge to happiness

H.S.H. Prince Honore III of Monaco was determined unlike his predecessors, to marry for love. He lost his heart to Catherine de Brignole, daughter of the former Doge of Genoa.

The marriage, after a great deal of planning, was very nearly cancelled at the last moment by the Bride's mother.

When she arrived from Genoa with Catherine in a galley, she insisted that the Bridegroom come aboard to collect her.

Honore however, as a Sovereign, refused to advance further than the landing stage. The Genoese flotilla turned round and sailed back to Bordighera, and the Prince was in despair.

It returned two days later because the Bride's uncle suggested a bridge should be built between the shore and the galley so the young couple could meet half way.

AUGUST

August 1st   1625

The Queen punished

After a meeting of the Privy Council, King Charles I sent for his Queen, the fifteen-year-old Henrietta Maria. She refused to come, pleading a toothache.

With the whole Privy Council following him, King Charles marched to her apartments. He found her servants 'unreverently dancing and cavorting in her presence.'

He stopped the party and declared that all her French servants would have to leave. Horror stricken, Henrietta Maria became hysterical, throwing herself on her knees and begging him to relent. But the King would not even allow his wife to say goodbye to her friends.

When the Queen saw the French men and women standing in the courtyard below, she broke the windows with her fists, screaming and calling out to them. The King dragged her back, her hands pouring with blood.

Later the King and Queen developed a deep mutual devotion and Henrietta Maria turned into what she said was "the happiest woman in the world."

August 2nd   1833

Saved from a falling mast

H.R.H. Princess Victoria wrote:

"At about ½ past 9 we went on board *dear little Emerald*. We were to be towed to Plymouth. Mama and Lehzen were very sick, and I was sick for about ½ an hour. At 1, I had a hot mutton chop on deck.

"We passed Dartmouth. At about 4 we approached Plymouth Harbour. It is a magnificent place and the breakwater is wonderful indeed. . . .

"As we entered the harbour, our dear little *Emerald* ran foul of a hulk, her mast broke and we were in the *greatest danger*. Thank God! the mast did not fall and no one was hurt: but I was *dreadfully* frightened for *Mama* and for *all*.

"The poor dear *Emerald* is very much hurt I fear. Saunders was not at all in fault; he saved us by pulling the rope which fixed us to the steamer. . . . My precious dog *Sweet Dash* was under Saunders's arm the whole time, but he never let him drop in all the danger."

August 3rd   1925

A costly Prince

The Indian Prince Bhupinder Singh, Maharajah of Patiala visited London and took over the entire fifth floor of the Savoy Hotel – comprising thirty-five suites.

His rooms were filled with 3,000 roses ordered fresh every day, a silver bath was installed for him and he had exclusive use of a private lift decorated in scarlet and gold laquer.

The 20 stone Prince was also said to wear special underpants costing £200 a pair.

August 4th   1900

The Lady Elizabeth Bowes-Lyon

The youngest daughter of Claude George Bowes-Lyon, 14th Earl of Strathmore was born at St. Paul's Walden to-day.

The baby girl was named Elizabeth after the Tudor Queen, Angela because her father regarded her as an angel, and Marguerite due to her mother's great love of flowers.

When Lady Elizabeth became the Duchess of York she met Velma the famous palmist who had predicted the Assassination of the Tzar of Russia.

'She told the Duchess:

"I see in your hand that your marriage will be so happy and successful, and will be made more successful still by the arrival of a child who will be worshipped from one end of the Empire to the other."

August 5th   1893

Trouble at Cowes

The Kaiser and the Prince of Wales, later King Edward VII, were at daggers drawn.

The Kaiser had brought with him to Cowes on the Isle of Wight a racing yacht *Meteor I* especially re-designed to beat his Uncle's *Britannia*, which it promptly did.

The Prince was furious and humiliated because he had always been the 'Boss' of Cowes.

He also smarted under the knowledge that his nephew had called him on an important occasion in Germany 'That Old Peacock'.

In retaliation he referred to him scornfully as 'William the Great'.

August 6th   1928

A great statesman is impressed

Winston Churchill was a guest of the King and Queen at Balmoral. He wrote to his wife:

"There is no one here at all except the family, the household and Princess Elizabeth – aged two. The latter is a character. She has an air of authority and reflectiveness astonishing in an infant."

August 7th   1902

The Shah's mistake

Legend has it that a visiting Shah of Persia, regarding Queen Alexandra's Ladies-in-Waiting and mistaking them for Edward VII's harem, exclaimed: "These are your wives? They are old and ugly. Have them beheaded and take new pretty ones."

On two counts the Shah was wrong: in the first place, Queen Alexandra delighted in showing herself off among handsome women and pretty girls.

Secondly the King never approached any of his wife's Ladies for their favours.

He dismissed her Maids of Honour as 'bread-and-butter Misses,' preferring the more experienced charms of such 'women of the world' as Lady Randolph Churchill and Mrs. Lillie Langtry.

August 8th   1761

Music rules the waves

Princess Charlotte of Mecklenburg-Strelitz arrived in England to marry H.M. King George III. On the voyage she played 'God Save the King' over and over again on her harpsichord.

All the English Lords and Ladies sent to accompany her were prostrated with sea-sickness but she managed to survive the voyage by being immersed in her music.

She was a little monkey-faced woman, which made it seem extraordinary that the King was a loving and faithful husband.

August 9th   1868

Royal orchids

Cora Pearl, one of the great Courtesans of the Second Empire in France, captured His Imperial Prince Napoleon, the Emperor's brother.

Their liaison lasted nine years, the longest known at the time.

On this day the Prince gave Cora 'a large vanload' of the most expensive orchids.

She dressed herself as a sailor and danced on them the hornpipe followed by the can-can.

August 10th   1901

Queen Alexandra enjoys motoring

The Queen's favourite pleasure was motoring.

She was most enthusiastic for this new form of locomotion, although as a passenger she must have been a little disconcerting.

"I did enjoy," she said, "being driven about in the cool of the evening at fifty miles an hour! I have the greatest confidence in our driver. I poke him violently in the back with my sunshade at every corner to make him go gently and whenever a dog, child or anything else crosses our way!"

August 11th   1100

A mysterious death

On this day H.M. King William II was mysteriously killed by an arrow while hunting in the New Forest.

Many writers in the twelfth century felt that this was an act of Divine vengeance for the savage methods his father King William had used when instituting the New Forest as his hunting preserve.

August 12th   1709

Comfortable retirement

H.M. King Stanislaus I of Poland was deposed by his people in 1709 after reigning for not quite five years.

They found him too expensive and too extravagant but even without the throne he was able to devote the remaining years of his life to luxurious living.

He settled down in Lorraine and had a household that consisted of 510 persons.

Included amongst these were 16 Gentlemen-of-the-Bedchamber, 4 Private Secretaries, 12 valets, 40 footmen, 31 porters and 10 masters of his horses.

He also paid 41 gardeners and 63 musicians.

August 13th   1673

The stubborn Princess

One day, walking together in the Park, two children, Princess
Mary and Princess Anne of York, saw in the distance what looked
like a man or a tree. Princess Anne was sure it was a tree.

Convinced it was a man, Princess Mary asked:

"Now, sister, are you satisfied what it is?"

Lady Anne, however, turned away after she saw what it was, and
determined to be right cried:

"No, sister, 'tis a tree!"

When she became Queen, Anne continued to be extremely
stubborn and would rarely listen to reasoned argument.

August 14th   1688–1740

Wise and brave

H.M. Frederick William II King of Prussia had an appalling
childhood owing to the cruelty of his father.

When he succeeded to the throne he established the most
cultivated Court in Europe. Although his father had not allowed
him to read or enjoy himself in any way, he had an intelligent
mind, and invited the greatest writers and philosophers of the age
to his Palace.

Among them was Voltaire the famous French author who was so
impressed with the king that he hailed him as 'The Solomon of the
North'.

But the King also proved to be a brave and outstanding military commander.

He led his army with great success in both the War of the Austrian Succession and the Seven Years' War.

It was these triumphs which earned him the title of 'Frederick the Great'.

August 15th   1630

An omen of blood

H.M. Charles I was sitting in the garden of Whitehall Palace. The famous sculpturer, Bernini, had finished a bust of him and had brought it to him there.

He was quite certain that His Majesty would admire it.

At the moment that he asked for it to be uncovered so that the King could see it in all its glory, a hawk flew by with a bird in its beak. A drop of the victim's blood fell onto the throat of the statue.

The King was beheaded by Cromwell as 'an implacable enemy of the Commonwealth of England'. Just before his execution he remembered the incident and the omen that it gave him of bad luck.

August 16th   1821

A Royal healer

H.R.H. Prince Leopold Alexander of Hohlenlohe had created a sensation in the 19th century in Europe by becoming a faith healer.

On this day he met a peasant who was also a Healer called Martin Michel, who took him to see Princess Mathilde Schwartzenberg who was a seventeen-year-old cripple.

To the amazement of everybody, she was healed and the citizens of Wurtzberg went crazy. The halt and the lame for miles began pouring into the city seeking health from the magical hands of the Royal Priest.

Many of the sick people became hysterical and the Prince was overwhelmed with sufferers of all manner of distressing conditions.

The papers reported cases of the blind seeing, the lame walking and the deaf hearing. Among them was none other than the Crown Prince of Bavaria, the future King Ludwig I.

But of course there were sceptics who said that the Prince had paid half a dozen men to hobble up to him and when he told them to throw away their sticks and walk, they did.

No-one to this days knows whether the Prince was really a healer or whether a great deal of his success was faith.

Nevertheless he retired and had a quiet life as a Churchman preaching and helping the needy and writing small books on devotional subjects.

In 1844 he was made a Bishop and five years later he died aged 55.

August 17th   1930

No change allowed

At Windsor, H.M. King George V's Sitting Room was the Blue Room where his grandfather had died, and the King wished it kept just as his father, Edward VII, had furnished it.

Nothing must be changed – the red leather chairs, the stiff sofa, the mahogany bookcase – all must be in the rightful places.

He was therefore infuriated when, not having been made aware of the King's wishes, a new house-maid 'put everything back wrong'.

Flying into a rage he sent for the Housekeeper and asked angrily why the girl should have done such a thing.

Apologising, the Housekeeper said:

"Be sure it'll never happen again, Your Majesty".

Then with sudden inspiration, she added:

"I'll get the room photographed".

The idea so pleased the King that he calmed down immediately – and the room *was* photographed.

August 18th   1661

Two loves

King Louis XIV, known as the Roi de Soleil, fell in love with Versailles and Louise de La Vallière at the same time.

Over the years he had many other loves but the splendour of his

Court and the genius of his age, made him the most unforgettable and glamorous King of European history.

On this date he finished building Versailles which was really more important to him than anything else he has ever done.

One of his Beauties Madame de Montespan had tried desperately hard to attract him and finally resorted to invoking Satan and Black Magic. What was more, she won!

August 19th   1463

The oak tree

H.M. King Edward IV, when out hunting, saw a very pretty woman under an oak tree waiting to speak to him.

When she did so, she begged him to restore her dead husband's lands to her sons. The King thought it was something that should be done, but while he was arranging it he fell in love with her.

He asked Elizabeth Woodville if she would be his mistress. She replied:

"My liege, I know I am not good enough to be your Queen, but I am far too good to be your mistress."

Because the King felt he could not live without her, they were married secretly, but in the following months he realised how important she was to his life and they announced that their marriage had taken place.

She was crowned, and it was a blissfully happy story which all started because she was brave enough to wait for the King under an oak tree.

August 20th   1885

H.R.H. Princess Victoria of Hesse

The Princess had already had her first child when Queen Victoria wrote:

"Let me again ask you to remember that your *firt duty* is to your dear and most devoted *Husband* to whom you can *never* be *kind enough* and to whom I think a *little* more tenderness is due *sometimes*. He is so good a son that I am sure his great wish will be to aid you in every way to be a comfort and support to poor dear Papa. You must watch over him and be *very particular yourself* as to *who* you see and make more intimate acquaintances with and in *this* dear Ludwig will surely help you. . . . .

"Ever your devoted and loving Grandmama

V.R.I."

August 21st   1889

The King abdicates

To-day H.M. King Alexander I of Bulgaria renounced his Rank and his Titles. The King, clever and attractive, was the son of Prince Alexander of Hesse and his morganatic wife who became Princess of Battenburg.

He was a great favourite of Queen Victoria and at the age of twenty-two was chosen to rule Bulgaria, one of the new Balkan States created by the Congress of Berlin in 1878.

In 1886 the Russians organised a Military conspiracy in Sofia forcing the King to sign his Abdication under fear of death. They handcuffed him and took him off to Russia.

Queen Victoria never forgave the Russians and the Bulgarians wept in the streets.

The King however fell madly in love with the beautiful, young, golden voiced, Louise Loisinger, the star of the Darmstadt Court Theatre.

He renounced his Rank and Titles to marry her in 1889.

His cousin the Grand Duke Louis IV of Hesse gave him the non-Royal title of Count Hartenau.

Wearing the grand crosses of thirty-six different orders, which Kings and Emperors had given him in his days of glory, he entered the Austrian Army as a Lieutenant Colonel.

August 22nd   1858

Telegrams!

The first Royal telegram crosses the Atlantic from Europe to America. H.M. Queen Victoria and President Buchanan exchanged compliments.

Her Majesty sent the following message:

'The Queen desires to congratulate the President upon the successful completion of this great international work, in which the Queen has taken the greatest interest. The Queen is convinced that the President will join with her in fervently hoping that the electric cable, which now connects Great Britain with the United States, will prove an additional link between the two nations, whose friendship is founded upon their common interests and reciprocal esteem . . . . .'

Unfortunately Queen Victoria's hopes were cruelly dampened as the cable ceased to function on the 3rd September.

It was not until 1866 that the link was re-established.

August 23rd   1359

A King's revenge

H.M. King Pedro I of Portugal had a corpse raised from the burial ground, dressed in robes, placed on a throne, and crowned as his Queen.

It was the climax of very harrowing sufferings during his youth.

His first fiancée was Edward III's daughter Princess Joan, but on her way to marry him, she was struck down by the Black Death.

He was extremely upset by this, but agreed to marry Constance of Castile. They were married for five years then she died in 1345.

Prince Pedro, however, found real happiness with Inez de Castro, and was very much in love with her.

However his father King Alfonso XI refused to allow them to marry. Pedro however was determined not to lose another woman whom he loved. He married Inez in secret at Braganza on New Year's Day 1355.

They lived very quietly, but the King began to suspect he was being deceived.

One day when Prince Pedro was out hunting he went to Inez and told her bluntly that he believed she was his daughter-in-law.

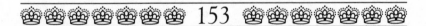

She begged for mercy, but as soon as the old King left three of his men broke into the villa and assassinated her and her three children.

When the murder was discovered Pedro vowed when he came to the throne he would seek revenge on the murderers.

His first act on ascending the throne was to order the execution of his wife's assassins. Only two could be found but they were brought back from Spain, tortured in front of the new King and finally had their hearts ripped from their bodies.

Two years later King Pedro ordered the corpse of his beloved wife Inez to be taken from its resting place in the Cathedral at Coimbra and taken to Alcobaca.

Here she was dressed in Royal robes, placed on a throne and solemnly crowned.

August 24th   1485

A King degraded

H.M. King Richard III was killed in the battle of Bosworth. His body was taken to Leicester and displayed in public for two days before being buried at Grey Friars.

Henry VII, the first Tudor King, erected a tomb to his defeated rival, but this was destroyed when the Grey Friars was dissolved by King Henry VIII.

King Richard's body was then flung into the River Soar.

August 25th   1554

The pearl of love

H.M. King Philippe of Spain gave his wife Mary Tudor of England the most perfect pearl in the world. It was the 'Perigrina' pearl which was the sister of the ear-ring that Queen Cleopatra dissolved in vinegar as an aphrodisiac for her lover Anthony.

It was found by a black slave in the Gulf of Panama, who won his freedom as a result.

At the time of Emperor Napoleon's occupation of Spain in 1808 the 'Perigrina' ear-ring disappeared.

Years after Napoleon's fall it was with the Spanish Royal Family, and it now belongs to the Duke of Abercorn.

There is an old legend that says:

"Tears of joy shed by the Angels for the ultimate destiny of man were the tears that fell into the pearl oyster shell."

August 26th   1790

A Royal experiment

H.M. Gustav of Sweden was an early campaigner against coffee which he was convinced was poisonous.

To prove this he decided to experiment on two convicted murderers. He sentenced one to drink coffee every day, and the other to drink only tea, with two Doctors to oversee the experiment.

The King was convinced he would have proof of the fatal effects of the dreaded beverage.

The first death was of one of the doctors, to be followed shortly by his colleague. The next was the King, murdered when attending the opera in Stockholm in 1792.

The condemned men kept on drinking until finally the first one died aged eighty-three.

He was the tea-drinker.

August 27th   1979

H. M. Queen Victoria's Great-Grandson is assassinated

It was August Bank Holiday. Admiral of the Fleet The Earl Mountbatten of Burma was holidaying with his family at his Castle on the West Coast of Ireland.

Six of them and Lord Mountbatten set off from Classiebawn in a motor cruiser *Shadow V* to lift the lobster pots they had set the day before.

Lord Mountbatten was in his place at the wheel and moved the cruiser out of harbour.

A few hundred yards from the shore five pounds of gelignite exploded under him. The boat was thrown high up into the air.

Lord Mountbatten was killed instantly, so was his grandson Nicholas and a young friend. The rest of the party were badly injured but alive.

A great man, a hero, the last Viceroy of India, First Sea Lord, Supreme Chief of Combined Operations – the Uncle, friend and admirer of all the Royal Family.

Lord Mountbatten died wearing the symbol of his most heroic action – the Kelly Jersey.

June 20th 1837

At six o'clock the young Princess Victoria received the Archbishop of Canterbury and Lord Conyingham at Kensingham Palace. She saw her visitors fall on their knees and learned that she was Queen.

June 26th 1830

H.M. King George IV died. Raffish, pleasure-seeking, flamboyant, extravagant, he maintained a secret loyalty to Mrs Fitzherbert.

July 7th 1789

H.R.H. King George III's Court moves to Weymouth. During the visit the King went for a dip in the sea. Miss Burney recorded '. . . a machine follows the Royal one into the sea, filled with fiddlers who play *God Save the King* as His Majesty takes the plunge!'

July 19th 1821

H.M. Queen Caroline was not a happy Queen. After the coronation of her husband, H.M. King George IV, the Royal Family and 312 men banqueted in Westminster Hall. The day was marred by the scandal of Queen Caroline attempting to storm the locked doors, to no avail. Her husband could not abide her.

August 10th 1901

H.M. Queen Alexandra's favourite pleasure was motoring. 'I did enjoy' she said 'being driven about in the cool of the evening at fifty miles an hour!'

August 25th 1554

H.M. Queen Mary was given the most magnificent pearl in the world by her husband King Philip of Spain. It was the 'Perigrina', found by a slave in the Gulf of Panama, who won his freedom as a result.

August 27th 1979

Lord Mountbatten was killed on the motor cruiser *Shadow V* off the coast of Ireland. A great man, a hero, Lord Mountbatten died wearing the symbol of his most heroic action, the Kelly Jersey.

September 7th 1553

H.M. Queen Elizabeth I was born at Greenwich. Chapuys wrote that it was 'to the great shame and confusion of Physicians, Astrologers, Wizards and Witches, all of whom had affirmed it would be a boy'.

August 28th   1609

A disappointed King

H.M. James I, King of England decided he would start a British silk-weaving industry.

He therefore imported 10,000 mulberry trees, and had them placed on the site in London where Buckingham Palace now stands.

Unfortunately the king did not know that there were two types of Mulberry trees. In one the silk-worms spun happily, in the other they would produce nothing.

Unfortunately King James had planted the wrong sort.

After several crop failures he took no further interest in the idea. The trees were felled, the land became a pleasure garden, and eventually the site of a Royal residence.

Today in the South-West corner of Buckingham Palace gardens stands one black mulberry tree. It is a memento of a King's unhappy silkworm experiment.

August 29th   1968

Love is victorious

H.R.H. Crown Prince Herald of Norway fell in love with Sonia Haraldsen, an Oslo Draper's daughter, when they were both teenagers. They had to fight fervently for several frustrating years until in 1968 the Marriage was allowed.

Now Crown Prince Harald is tall, very good-looking and exceedingly popular. His pretty wife adores him.

The Norwegians say proudly:

"She belongs to the people!"

August 30th   1594

The Christening of H.R.H. Prince Henry of Scotland

The ceremony had been delayed time after time since the Prince's birth in February.

The Chapel Royal at Stirling where King James himself had been baptised was much too small for a Christening planned on such a lavish scale, and the King set to work to enlarge it.

Splendid Pageants and rich Banquets were planned with which King James hoped to dazzle the world. It was by no means easy.

The King was so poor and his plate so scanty that when he invited Sir Walter Dundas to the Christening he begged him to bring 'his silver spoons'.

The Dutch Ambassador's present consisted, among other things, of several heavy gold cups; shortly afterwards these were melted down as yet another effort to increase the King's purse.

August 31st   1880

A Queen's unquenchable spirit

A daughter was born to King William III of the Netherlands and his second wife Emma.

Christened Wilhelmina, the child became the Queen, and during World War I she was influential in maintaining neutrality of her country.

When Germany invaded the Netherlands in 1940 Wilhelmina fled to England with her family and encouraged her people's morale through her Radio Broadcasts.

She exhorted them to maintain their spirit until the nation was liberated. After the German occupation she was welcomed back with great enthusiasm.

SEPTEMBER

September 1st   1715

To meet in eternity

Louis XIV of France died. He had reigned over France for seventy-two years. As he lay dying he said to his wife, Madame de Maintenon:

"What consoles me in quitting you, is the hope that we shall soon be reunited in eternity."

She made no reply to this farewell but is reported to have said as she left the room:

"See the appointment which he makes with me! This man has never loved any one but himself."

September 2nd   1666

At his Royal best

H.M. King Charles II was always at his best in a crisis. As the Great Fire of London broke out, most of the people in Whitehall started to load their valuables into a row-boat on the Thames.

King Charles rode into the City on horseback. The authorities had completely lost their heads and he took command.

He directed the blowing up of houses and arranged for the care of the destitute.

Toiling ceaselessly with the troops to fight the flames, His Majesty passed buckets with his own hands.

"It is not imaginable how extraordinary the vigilance of the King was," an eye witness observed.

September 3rd   1589

Peril of a Royal bride

James VI's bride to be, the fourteen-year-old Anne of Denmark, embarked for Scotland, but the gales were so strong in the North Sea that she was driven back to take shelter in Norway.

When news of the delay reached Scotland, the King set out to meet her but was himself driven back into harbour by the bad weather.

Only on the second attempt did His Majesty reach the coast of Norway.

The couple were married in Denmark and remained there until the Spring, when, crossing to Scotland at last, they were troubled again by high seas.

Many people believed that there were witches at work in Scotland, who, in conjunction with their sisterhood in Norway, had brewed the storms to drown the young Queen.

September 4th   1850

The Queen is unknown

Because of Queen Victoria's unpretentious mode of dress, she was sometimes mistaken for an ordinary tourist.

During her first stay at Holyrood House she wandered about like an ordinary visitor – and was mistaken for one.

She wrote in her diary:

"I saw the rooms where Queen Mary of Scots lived, her bed, the Dressing Room into which the murderers entered to kill Rizzio, and the spot where he fell. It was there that the old Housekeeper said to me:

'If the lady would stand on that side, she would see that the boards are discoloured by his blood.'

The old Housekeeper did not know who I was!"

September 5th   1971

A Royal victory

H.R.H. The Princess Anne won the European Horse Trials at Burghley.

The Times reported:

"With only three years of necessarily spasmodic experience behind her, Princess Anne today reached the highest pinnacle of equestrian achievement which she has so far attempted."

The Queen and the Duke of Edinburgh had watched anxiously from the stands as their daughter rode to victory on *Doublet* which had been a Christmas present from Her Majesty the year before.

Princess Anne was named Sports Personality of the Year by B.B.C. viewers.

September 6th   1640

The Sultan who killed

Murad IV Sultan of the Ottoman Empire was a killer. He enjoyed killing people and on this day in 1635 he had 75,000 subjects executed.

He would go out in disguise to look for people who were doing something wrong, or whom he objected to, and had them killed by Kara Ali his Chief Executioner.

People who smoked, which was forbidden, especially when it was done in public, were sought out by the Sultan.

If he found someone smoking he would throw off his disguise and have them executed on the spot.

One day he found one of his gardeners and his wife puffing away secretly. He ordered their legs to be amputated and the two people were wheeled through the streets until they bled to death.

In 1640 after a long drinking bout Murad died aged only 28. But even as he realised he could no longer live he ordered his brother Ibrahim who was his successor to be murdered.

When his mother told him the order had been carried out Murad smiling sank back on his cushions and died.

Actually his mother had been lying and the murderer Murad was succeeded by his brother Ibrahim.

He was the first man to survive his brother's blood thirsty sentences of death.

September 7th   1553

Royal predictions wrong

Queen Elizabeth I was born at Greenwich today.

H.M. Henry VIII had been born there as was his daughter Mary.
The announcement read:

'Queen Anne was brought to bed of a fair daughter at three of the
clock in the afternoon.'

The King had been convinced that Anne was to give birth to a
boy, but Chapuys wrote:

"The King's mistress was delivered of a girl, to the great
disappointment and sorrow of His Majesty and of the Lady herself,
and of others of her party. Also to the great shame and confusion of
Physicians, Astrologers, Wizards and Witches, all of whom had
affirmed it would be a boy."

September 8th   1761

*H.R.H. the Princess of Mecklenburg arrives at St. James's Palace to
meet her future husband George III*

Mr Hedley wrote:

"Her Royal Highness looked up and bowed. Her appearance to
me was easy, genteel and agreeable, but not handsome. Her head
was dressed and lapets down her neglegee was silver stuff trimed
with thin gold lace. . . . .

Lord Harcourt jumped out as the coach was going on to be ready to attend her Lord Anson did the same and fell down that the wheel was near going over him. . ."

The Princess threw herself at the King's feet, he raised her up, embraced her and led her through the garden up the steps into the Palace.

September 9th   1087

Words of the wise

Before he died on this day, H.M. King William the Conqueror of England had speculated on the fate of his sons after his death.

The wise men of his Court planned a way of discovering what the future might hold in this respect. They asked each one the question:

"If God had made you a bird, what bird would you wish to have been?"

Robert Curthose answered:

"A hawk, because it resembles most a courteous and gallant Knight."

William Rufus's answer to the same question was:

"I would be an eagle, because it is a strong and powerful bird, and feared by all other birds, and therefore it is kind over them all."

Lastly came the younger brother, Henry, and his choice was a starling:

"Because it is a debonnaire and simple bird, and gains its living without injury to any one, and never seeks to rob or grieve its neighbour."

The wise men returned immediately to the King.

Robert, they said, would be bold and valiant, and would gain renown and honour, but he would finally be overcome by violence, and die in prison. William would be powerful and strong as the eagle, but feared and hated for his cruelty and violence, until he ended a wicked life by a bad death. But Henry would be wise, prudent, and peaceful, unless when actually compelled to engage in war, and would die in peace after gaining wide possessions.

So when King William lay on his death-bed he remembered these words and bequeathed Normandy to Robert, England to William, and his own treasures, without land to his younger son Henry, who eventually became King.

September 10th   1898

The Empress of Austria assassinated

One of the most beautiful women in the world, Elizabeth Empress of Austria, was today stabbed to the heart by an Italian Anarchist where she was walking from her Hotel in Geneva to the Steamboat Pier.

Her Majesty was then taken back to her Hotel and died a little later.

A brilliant rider, adored by the people of Hungary who made her their Queen, she was unhappy in Austria due to the stiff restriction of the Hapsburg Court.

Despite his infidelities and the Empress's long absences from Vienna, the Emperor Franz Joseph had always loved her.

September 11th   1868

Plain, shy, pious, frumpish Princess Louise marries H.R.H. Crown Prince Frederick of Denmark

Prince Frederick had been known in his childhood as 'Freddie with the pretty face'. He was assured, elegant, charming, cheerful and very good looking.

At twenty-five he was a very eligible bachelor and everyone expected him to make a brilliant marriage.

To the astonishment of all, in 1868 he became engaged to seventeen-year-old Princess Louise, the only child of the King of Sweden.

Everyone thought her plain and frumpish, yet amazingly Freddie loved her and they were ecstatically happy. They had seven children.

September 12th   1494

A kingly King

Francis I of France was born the son of Charles Angoulême and Louise de Savoy. When Louis XII became King in 1498 Francis became heir presumptive to the throne and was made Duke of Valois.

Francis became King when he was just twenty-one. He was a giant, over two metres tall, with a large hook nose, low forehead and bulbous eyes. The magnificence of his clothes, the close fitting doublets, tight at the waist and with large skirts, with slashed sleeves, the tights and extravagant shoes, the feathered hats, drew the crowds' notice to his physical appearance.

September 13th   1940

The Queen says no

When there was every likelihood of the Germans invading England, Her Majesty Queen Elizabeth was asked if it would not be safer to retreat overseas. She smiled sweetly and replied:

"The Princesses cannot go without me. I cannot go without the King. The King will never go."

The King's view when asked was:

"Not Pygmalion likely!"

When Buckingham Palace was bombed the Queen said:

"I'm almost comforted that the Palace has been hit. Now I feel I can look the blitzed East End in the face."

September 14th   1762

Empress of Russia

No one believed the Empress's announcement that her deposed husband Peter II had died of colic. She was, the Foreign Embassies said:

"A murderess, a usurper and a whore."

On the day of her Coronation she made her lover, Gregory Orlov her Adjutant-General, gave him the title of Count and presented him with her portrait set in diamonds which he wore over his heart.

The French Charge d'Affaires reported –

"Scorning etiquette, he takes liberties with his Sovereign in public which in polished Society no self-respecting mistress permits in her lover."

In private, Orlov beat Catherione, and she fell more deeply in love with "the handsomest man I have ever seen."

September 15th   1847

All things to all men

Carlo Lodovico, Duke of Lucca was an amusing and original character. He had estates in Saxony, and he would retire there whenever he was weary of Court Life.

There he became a Protestant.

"When I go to Constantinople I shall be a Mohammedan," he told scandalised Spiritual advisers, "in fact, wherever I go I always adopt, for the time being, the religion of the country as it keeps me so much more in tone with the local colour-scheme."

He was very erratic and had a roving eye, being intensely bored by his plain and pious wife.

September 16th   1892

An American Queen

On this day the first American married a reigning European Sovereign.

Alice Heine was the widow of the Duc de Richelieu. She was beautiful, accomplished and a great patron of the Arts. When she met H.S.H. Prince Albert I of Monaco they fell in love.

The Prince's first marriage to an English girl, daughter of the eleventh Duke of Hamilton, was a failure from the start. He and the bride has been forced into marriage by their parents and Napoleon III.

The new Princess of Monaco made the small Principality a centre for Opera, Ballet and the Theatre.

Alas, her happiness with her husband only lasted for ten years.

September 17th   1701

A King in exile

H.M. King James II hurriedly returned to France after an unsuccessful campaign to regain his throne culminating with the Battle of the Boyne in 1690.

King Louis XIV gave him a pension of a million *livres* a year, as he remained in exile until his death. Gloomy and penitent, he was mystified by the ways of God, whose agent he truly believed himself to be.

September 18th   1714

A King arrives

The Elector of Hanover, now styled George I of Great Britain, landed at Greenwich. He was fifty-four years of age and a foreigner, yet he was received in London with all external demonstrations of honour.

Two hundred coaches of Nobles and officials preceded his own. The city authorities met him at St Margaret's Hill, Southwark, in all their paraphernalia, to congratulate him on his taking possession of his Kingdom.

September 19th   1356

A desperate battle

The Black Prince defeated the French at the Battle of Poitiers. The English were overwhelmingly outnumbered, and they had unexpectedly encountered the French force whilst returning from another expedition.

"God help us!" the Black Prince exclaimed; and then added dauntlessly: "We must consider how we can best fight them."

The French army was routed but King John the Good valiantly continued the fight. After a desperate struggle he was taken prisoner by the English, along with his son Philip.

September 20th   1936

A King is cruel

When H.M. King Edward VIII had fallen in love with Mrs. Wallis Simpson, he dismissed Mrs. Dudley Ward, his Mistress of many years, in a very cruel way.

She had been away with her family and returning to London she rang up the King at St. James's Palace as she always did.

To her surprise there was a silence from the telephonist and then the girl burst into tears.

"What is the matter?" Mrs Ward enquired.

"I have been told when you ring not to put you through to His Royal Highness!" she sobbed.

September 21st   1856

Lady with the lamp

Queen Victoria met Florence Nightingale at Balmoral. The Queen had been aware of her famed reputation in the Crimea for some time.

In January Her Majesty had written Miss Nightingale a letter praising her work and enclosed a brooch:

"The form and emblems of which commemorate your great and blessed work, and which, I hope, you will wear as a mark of the high approbation of your Sovereign."

The brooch was inscribed with 'Blessed are the Merciful', and it bore a St George's Cross in red enamel, besides the Royal cypher surmounted by a crown in diamonds.

The Queen was enchanted to meet "a gentle ladylike person with short hair who must have been very pretty before her Crimean experiences."

September 22nd   1870

The Dream King

On this day Ludwig II of Bavaria had his first plan for the Linderhof, which was to become the most beloved of all his Fairy Palaces.

He had come to the throne at the age of eighteen and his people knew they had the most strikingly handsome young Sovereign in Europe.

He promised a new age of glory in Bavaria, but he lived in a dream-world and his Castle and Palaces became more fantastic, one after the other, and gradually ceased to amuse his Subjects when they cost so much money.

Linderhof, which was spoken of as 'the most opulent one-bedroom residence in the whole world', was exquisite outside. But Ludwig's fancies extended to a Grotto which proceeded down a cave hung with 'stalactites' made of cast iron, and ended in a lake which was fed by a waterfall.

He could change the colours of the water by turning a switch and ripple the lake's surface into artificial waves.

As Ludwig grew older there were more and more grumbles and complaints about his wild extravagance – like having seventeen carvers working full time for four-and-a-half years on one bedroom in the Neauschwanstein.

They were not to know that after they eventually tried to certify him as insane, his fairy-tale Castles were to become the greatest tourist draw of Bavaria, and give pleasure and delight to thousands of people who visit them from all over the world.

September 23rd   1326

The invasion of England

Queen Isabella of England left Flanders with an Army to conquer England. She was the first foreigner with troops to do so since William the Conqueror in 1066.

Queen Isabella with her lover Roger Mortimer had dethroned her husband Edward II, a homosexual, to put her son on the throne.

Roger Mortimer was anxious to kill King Edward but he did not wish to be known as a murderer.

King Edward was trapped at Neath Abbey after an abortive attempt to escape by sea. His male lover was castrated and then hung fifty feet in the air. Then King Edward was dragged to Kenilworth Castle where he was made to give up his Great Seal.

The new reign of King Edward III was proclaimed on January 25th 1327.

The old King, who was now known as 'Lord Edward', was given jailors who were rustics and only knew country ways. They planned to kill with diseases contracted from filth. They placed bug-infested straw in his hair, releasing slimy insects to crawl on his scalp. scalp.

They shaved him with foul-smelling polluted ditch water but he clamped his lips shut and none entered his mouth.

They threw him into a moat with the putrid carcasses of dead cattle. 'Their stink was overwhelming but he did not sicken.'

Determined to eliminate 'Lord Edward', Mortimer now sent two sophisticated torturers to Berkeley Castle. They were given strict orders that no incriminating mark was to be found on 'Lord Edward's' body.

On September 21st an announcement was made that the father of the King was dead. The villagers round Berkeley Castle heard his piteous screams. One villager declared that the fire iron, which was called a *broche* was thrust into him through a plumber's tube or 'horn'.

This was a form of execution practised in mediaeval France known as *Supplice du Pal*.

September 24th   1561

Love in the Tower of London

H.M. Queen Elizabeth's Lady of the Bedchamber, Lady Catherine Grey, had secretly married the Earl of Hertford, Protector Somerset's eldest son, in December 1560 while the Queen was hunting at Eltham.

When Queen Elizabeth discovered that Lady Catherine was pregnant she sent her to the Tower and her son Edward was born on 24th September 1561. Later when the Earl of Hertford returned from a Diplomatic mission to France, he too was sent to the Tower.

There was no question of a Royal pardon. Catherine and the Earl remained in the Tower, but it was easy to bribe the gaolers for their meetings and soon Catherine was pregnant again.

She kept it secret and it was only on the birth of her second son, Thomas, in February 1563 that it came to light.

Catherine Grey and the Earl of Hertford never met again. She died on 22nd January 1568. Hertford was later set free to live to a comfortable old age and remarry twice.

September 25th   1613

Poor Jewel

Queen Anne, wife of James V, shooting at a deer, mistook her mark and killed Jewel, who was the King's principal and most special hound. His Majesty was extremely angry for a while, but when he discovered that it had been the Queen's fault he was soon pacified.

He told her not to be too upset and that he would not love her any less.

The next day he sent her a diamond worth £2,000, as a legacy from Jewel, his dead dog.

September 26th   1859

The Queen is Weight Conscious

When Queen Victoria was visiting Balmoral she liked to spend as much time as possible out of doors. There was beautiful scenery and outdoor pursuits for relaxation.

'No Queen,' Victoria wrote, 'has ever enjoyed what I am fortunate enough to enjoy.'

'When we were going down Craig-na-Ban,' she continued, 'which is very steep, and rough, Jane Churchill fell and could not get up again, (having got her feet caught in her dress) and John Brown (who is our factotum and really the perfection of a servant for he thinks of everything) picked her up like *un scene de tragedie* and when she thanked him, he said:

"Your Ladyship is not so heavy as Her Majesty!" which made us laugh. I said:

"Am I grown heavier do you think?"

"Well, I think you are," was the plain spoken reply.

"So I mean to be weighed as I always thought I was light!"

September 27th   1889

Royal rockets

His Majesty George III hunted in Windsor Forest, and in the evening went to the Observatory at the Tower.

He wished to view by night-glasses the process of a grand experiment, which was put to trial at Shooter's Hill and Nettlebed, by two experienced engineers.

The idea was the ability of conveying situative signals, at that time of night, between Army and Army.

His Majesty expressed great satisfaction at what he saw.

The Royal terrace at Windsor was crowded in the expectation of a grand exhibition of Fireworks, which were expected to have been let off at St Ann's Hill;

The company were most disappointed when they saw only a few rockets, in order to give his Majesty an opportunity of viewing them through a new-invented telescope!

September 28th   1635

"No" to the King

King Louis XIII of France had several mistresses but the relationship was invariably platonic. When one day Mlle de Hautefort, who lasted the longest of all his loves, coyly dropped a letter into her bosom, the King retrieved it with a pair of tongs.

In the autumn of 1635 King Louis XIII met Mlle de La Fayette who was a sixteen-year-old Maid of Honour with brown ringlets and blue eyes. A deeply pious girl, she refused and made the Sign of the Cross when Louis paid her the unheard-of compliment of asking her come and live with him at Versailles.

Mlle de La Fayette clearly detested the Cardinal de Richelieu and it was he who ordered her confessor to encourage her leaning towards the religious life. In May 1637 Louise entered a Carmelite convent in Paris, the King was in tears and she wept: "I shall never see him again."

Her confessor told the King that her decision could be postponed, but Louis replied that if he kept her from her vocation he would regret it all his life.

For a few months he visited Louise at her convent, though he was only able to speak to her through a grille. A somewhat worldly Abbess said that the King ought to exercise his Royal prerogative and come inside, but he was shocked by this suggestion.

The King died in May 1643. Acting on his instructions, an attendant removed the crucifix, which Louis wore on a cord round his neck, and took it to Louise, who had become Soeur Angelique.

September 29th   1588

Michelmas Day

H.M. Queen Elizabeth is said to have been eating her Michelmas goose when she received the joyful tidings of the defeat of the Spanish Armada.

September 30th   1927

H.R.H. Princess Elizabeth waves to her grandfather

When T.R.H. the Duke and Duchess of York were away on tour Princess Elizabeth stayed with her grandfather H.M. King George V at Buckingham Palace.

On their return their Highnesses moved into 145 Piccadilly, and King George found that with the aid of binoculars he could, from Buckingham Palace, see into the Nursery windows.

He would wait, watching patiently, until his granddaughter waved to him.

OCTOBER

October 1st   1216

A dish of pears

H.M. King John died and all England rejoiced. King John had
never expected to come to the throne. When he did he was a
faithless son, a faithless brother and a wicked uncle. It was
genuinely believed at the time that he killed with his own hands
the boy Arthur of Brittany, whose claims to the throne were better
than his own.

John was a notorious lecher and when he suspected his wife,
without any reason, of taking a lover, he had the man hanged and
his corpse suspended over her bed.

He was on his way to Newark when he felt slightly unwell, but he
pushed on and came to an Abbey where he stayed.

A monk named Simon was so incensed by the King's behaviour
that he went to the Abbot and said that if he would be absolved he
would give the King something to eat which would make 'all
England glad'.

Simon presented the King with a fine dish of pears, all but three
of which he had pricked with a poisoned needle.

The King asked him to share the dish, which he did, taking the
unpricked fruit. The King died and all England celebrated.

October 2nd   1771

The Royal Marriage Act

H.R.H. Henry Frederick, Duke of Cumberland, younger brother of H.M. George III, married the Honourable Mrs Horton.

Horace Walpole described her as 'A young widow of twenty-four, extremely pretty and well-made, and remarkable for the length of her eye-lashes, which veiled a pair of the most artful and coquettish eyes.'

King George III was furious when he found out.

It was this alliance and the marriage of the Duke of Gloucester to the Dowager Countess of Waldegrave, which followed shortly afterwards, that led to the passing of the Royal Marriage Act.

This Act subsequently rendered null the unions of George IV and the Duke of Sussex.

October 3rd   1468

Arrested by his vassal

On this day Charles the Bold, Duke of Burgundy, arrested H.M. King Louis XI at the Castle of Peronne, subjected him to close confinement and was even on the point of proceeding to further extremities.

But ultimately he was satisfied by dictating to King Louis a very humiliating treaty.

His Majesty was so mortified that on his return home he ordered to be killed a number of tame magpies who had been taught to cry: 'Peronne!'

October 4th   1561

A persistent poet

A Masque was held at Holyrood in which eight ladies dressed as men and eight men dressed as ladies.

Mary Queen of Scots wore a white doublet, black satin breeches and a pink silk mask.

Her partner, in a petticoat held out by a hoop, was the young poet Chastelard, who during the fun demanded that his 'husband' give him a kiss.

Laughingly, Queen Mary obliged.

In the belief that the kiss was a promise of greater favours, he hid himself in the Queen's sleeping apartment where he was discovered by her attendants.

Furious at his assumption, she banished the passionate poet from her Court.

Instead of being thankful for having escaped so lightly, Chastelard followed the Court to St Andrews where he entered Mary's bedchamber and attempted to make love to her in front of two Ladies-in-Waiting.

The Queen screamed for help, and when her half-brother, James Stewart, rushed in, she ordered him to run his sword through the intruder.

Instead Chastelard was brought to trial, found guilty of plotting against the Queen and beheaded.

October 5th   1263

A Royal raid

H.R.H. Prince Edward, later H.M. King Edward I, makes the first Royal bank-raid.

Finding himself unable to pay off his troops after a campaign in Wales, he remembered that the wealthy Knights Templars held his mother's jewellery in pawn.

He went to the Temple and told the Master there that he wished to see if the Royal jewels were safe, and was conducted to the Treasury which many people used like a modern safe deposit vault.

Here the Prince broke open the Merchants' coffers, took cash totalling £10,000 together with valuables which had been pledged against loans, and Queen Eleanor's jewels which he arrogantly carried off to Windsor.

His mother was in no way shocked. She merely pawned the jewels a second time with the King of France.

October 6th   1930

A surprise win

King Zog of Albania's one vice was gambling. This evening some English businessmen were playing poker in their hotel room when suddenly a policeman burst in.

They had been observed gambling, he explained.

The King himself had spotted them from a Palace window through a powerful pair of binoculars.

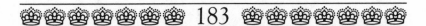

The men prepared themselves for the worst as the policeman continued:

"If you have nothing else lined up this evening, would you like to join His Majesty for a game?"

October 7th   1290

The Maid of Norway

H.R.H. The Princess Margaret became the infant Queen of Scotland in 1286, the last of the line of Scottish Rulers descended from King Malcolm III Canmore.

On this day her great-uncle King Edward I of England, arranged a marriage between Margaret and his son Edward, later King Edward II of England.

On the voyage from Norway to England, however, Queen Margaret fell ill and died.

She was only eight years old.

October 8th   1200

H.M. King John and Queen Isabella crowned

H.R.H. Prince John, the youngest child of Henry Plantaganet and Eleanor Duchess of Aquitaine, was destined for the Church.

At the moment of his accession, however, he fell passionately in love with Isabella, who was aged twelve and engaged to Hugh IX, the Lord of Lusignan.

King John swept Isabella into his arms and carried her off to England, where they were today married and crowned.

Hugh le Brun was so furious that he started a war which ended in King John losing most of his Continental possessions.

The King and Queen had two sons and three daughters, but King John also had five illegitimate children. Isabella loved him, despite his infidelity.

Besides King John's love of jewellery, much of which was lost in the quicksands of the Wash, he was very partial to eggs and ordered five-thousand for his Christmas festivities in 1206.

October 9th   1554

A Royal roving eye

Soon after their marriage H.M. King Philip of Spain began to complain that Mary Tudor was not attractive to him as she lacked 'all sensibility of the flesh'.

It was not long before rumours of his amorous adventures were rife in London and it was said that His Majesty preferred:

'The Baker's daughter in her russet gown,
Better than Queen Mary without her crown.'

It was this frustration which supplied the only touch of slapstick in the whole tragedy when at Hampton Court Palace Lady Magdalen Dacre was at her toilette.

Through the small window of her dressing-room the King espied the Lady-in-Waiting in an intriguing state of undress.

The first she knew of the interest she had aroused was when a groping hand, followed by an arm squeezed through the aperture.

Recognising the King's arm she nevertheless defended her modesty by seizing a staff and giving the offending limb a hearty blow whereupon the arm withdrew, as if by magic!

October 10th   1848

The King and the innkeeper

On one occasion during his exile in England, King Louis Philippe of France was wandering on foot through Twickenham, when he was accosted by a retired inn-keeper.

"Surely you remember me, Your Majesty," the man said, pumping his hands, "I kept the Crown."

Only a foreigner could have been so British in his reply: "That's more than I did."

October 11th   1216

Lost in the Wash

To reach Swineshead Abbey, H.M. King John had to cross the old River Ouse which flowed out into the Wash.

His Majesty's baggage train carrying his treasure and jewels followed slowly behind.

The plan was to negotiate the mouth of the River estuary, which was 4½ miles wide, at low tide. But in the autumn mists which hung over the fenlands the wagons lost their way, were trapped in the quicksands and overwhelmed by a rush of waters returning from the sea.

King John himself awaited his wagons on the Northern side of the River, but when he rode back to help, he found there was nothing he could do.

The ground opened in the midst of the waters and whirlpools sucked in everything – men and horses.

October 12th   632

Northumbria's first Christian Monarch

H.M. King Edwin the Great, the most powerful English Ruler of his day was converted to Christianity as a result of his marriage to Princess Aethelburh of Kent.

It was she who brought the Roman Missionary Paulinus to Northumbria.

King Edwin was slain in battle in 633.

October 13th   1683

Secret marriage of the Sun King

Starting by becoming Governess to King Louis's illegitimate children, in 1674 Madame de Maintenon began her long struggle for the King's soul.

Although the King took Mistress after Mistress, he was always at ease with her.

Her brilliant blue eyes and her intelligence was a pleasure every time he saw her and finally he fell in love.

Nineteen years after their secret marriage when Madame de Maintenon was sixty-seven, she wrote to the Bishop of Chartes saying that she was extremely tired and asking whether she could refuse to go to bed with the King twice a day.

She wrote:

"These painful occasions are now too much for me."

The Bishop, however, replied that she must obey her husband's wishes.

October 14th   1066

The Battle of Hastings

The battle began at about nine in the morning when William of Normandy sent forward his infantry to attack the English led by H.M. King Harold.

Initially the Norman attackers were thrust back and they were compelled to retreat.

It looked as if the English had won the day. But later King Harold was killed, struck down by a mounted Knight with his sword. With the loss of their Monarch the English took flight.

The battle had gone on all day and as darkness fell William called off the pursuit, encamping on the site of battle.

King Harold's body was found and buried, unconsecrated, on a cliff high above the seashore.

October 15th   1915

H.M. King George V visits his troops

H.M. King George makes five visits to the Western Front, those of 1914 passing off without incident.

But that of October 1915 was dramatic.

Having inspected his troops three cheers were given, so heartily that His Majesty's horse took fright.

It crouched on the ground, then reared straight up in the air. Its hind legs slipping it fell right on top of the King.

For three minutes he lay quite still, then he opened his eyes and asked for help to get up.

That was a mistake, for he had a double fracture of the pelvis and should have remained still until a doctor arrived.

It was essential that the degree of injury and the length of stay in France be kept a secret.

If the German spies had found out, the Château in which the King was staying would undoubtedly have been bombed.

It was not until early November that a Hospital train took the King to Boulogne.

Thereafter he suffered a recurring pain and this played upon his nerves and his temper.

He had always been irascible, but now his outbursts were more marked.

He was never to be the same man again – in fact the accident aged him by years.

October 16th   1855

Love at first sight

On this date the Emperor Napoleon III rode into Paris on a magnificent chestnut charger which he had brought from London.

Watching him being wildly acclaimed by the crowd was Eugenie de Montijo from Spain.

At that moment she lost her heart and decided that he was the man she would marry.

They met at a Hunt at Fontainbleau for which the Emperor had provided Eugenie with a mount.

By the end of the day it was obvious she had captured the Emperor and he was in love.

He pursued her relentlessly, but as the British Ambassador said:

"She played her game so well that he can get her no other way but by marriage."

Napoleon had been planning that a niece of Queen Victoria should be his Empress.

Finally, wildly in love, he battled with the almost impossible task of persuading his Ministers to accept Eugenie.

They were married in January 1883 and Queen Victoria wrote:

'The future Bride is beautiful, clever, very coquette, passionate and wild.'

For a short time they were ecstatically happy, but Napoleon's frequent desires were uncontrollable. He craved new eyes, new shapes, new sexual experiences.

Eugenie was not, however, prepared to play sweet music on a second string.

October 17th   1484

The Princes in the Tower

The Sixth Prince of Wales became Edward V for two brief months. He was twelve years old.

With his brother, George Duke of Gloucester, nine years old, he was imprisoned in the Tower of London by the wicked Richard of Gloucester, later Richard III.

They were there for five weeks. George wanted to learn to dance, but Edward said:

"It would be better to learn to die, for I think we are not long for this world."

The two murderers, Forest and Deighton entered their bed-room.

Edward was asleep, but George called out:

"Ha! Wake, for they have come to kill you!"

He then said to the Executioners:

"Why do you kill my brother? Kill me and let him live."

But they were both killed and their bodies cast into a secret place.

October 8th   1330

An amorous guest

King Edward III realised that the time had come to overthrow Sir Roger Mortimer who had been responsible for the death of his father.

He was also his mother's lover and regarded the King as a puppet.

Queen Isabella and Sir Roger were then living at Nottingham Castle, which was a huge fortress protected by a small Army.

King Edward decided to strike from within and on this day two dozen of his own men penetrated the stronghold by means of a secret passage which ran through the rock under the Castle.

Edward was waiting for them and they burst into the Queen's chamber and, ignoring her cries, seized Mortimer the Earl of March.

He was later sentenced to death, having been found guilty of murdering King Edward I and usurping the authority of King Edward II.

Tactfully, no mention was made of his liaison with his Royal mistress.

October 19th   1889

The best of the best

H.M. King Carlos of Portugal, a little fat man, succeeded his father, King Luis I, today.

He loved to be the best at everything he was doing, trying to be brilliant at a number of different things like billiards and painting.

He would proudly tell everyone he met of his reputation for being cleverer than his contemporaries.

He was actually a very good shot and was invited regularly to Windsor Castle to stay with the King.

If he thought anyone was looking at him, he would shoot from both shoulders alternately, then taking the gun in his hand like a pistol he would shoot low pheasants holding the gun stretched out in front of him.

In 1908 he was assassinated.

October 20th   1714

In the congregation

Westminster Abbey is packed for the Coronation of H.M. King George I. Lady Cowper wrote in her diary:

"One may easily conclude this was not a Day of real Joy to the Jacobites. However they were all there, looking as cheerful as they could, but very peevish with Everybody that spoke to them. My Lady Dorchester stood underneath me; and when the Archbishop went round the Throne, demanding the consent of the People, she turned to me and said:

"Does the old Fool think that Anybody here will say No to his Question, when there are so many drawn swords?"

A former mistress of King James II saw the Duchess of Portsmouth who has been one of King Charles I's mistresses and Lady Orkney who has been the same for King William IV, and exclaimed:

"Good God, who would have thought we whores would have been together here!"

October 21st   1973

H.M. Queen Elizabeth in Australia

H.M. Queen Elizabeth II opened the Sydney Opera House. *The Times* reported:

"The Queen opened the Sydney Opera House yesterday, launching a giant 'ship of sail' amid a great spectacle of carnival and colour.

More than one-million spectators crammed the foreshores of Sydney Harbour for the day-long festivities. It was a warm, but windy Spring day."

The Opera House took fourteen years to build and cost 62 million pounds.

Before a crowd of 15,000 invited guests and a globe-wide television audience estimated at 300-million, the Queen said that the Opera House captured the imagination of the world.

October 22nd   1954

In love at sixteen

Prince Juan Carlos was a guest on the King of Greece's yacht on a cruise in the Mediterranean.

He was sixteen, and another guest was Princess Sofia who was a year younger.

She was so beautiful that they fell in love, but they did not meet again until the Olympics in Rome in 1960, where Princess Sofia was watching her brother Prince Constantine win an Olympic gold medal for sailing.

The following year they met in York at the Duke of Kent's wedding, where they were both guests.

They knew then that they could not live without each other and Juan Carlos asked the King's permission to marry Sofia.

They had two marriage ceremonies – one Catholic and one Greek Orthodox.

Prince Juan Carlos was groomed to become General Franco's successor, and his reign began in October 1975 with a solemn High Mass in Madrid.

After forty-four years, Spain had a King again, and a Queen who was as beautiful as he was handsome.

October 23rd   1688

Spiteful gossip and a warming pan

King James II felt obliged to make a Declaration 'Enrolled in Chancery' that the birth of his son James Francis Edward was witnessed.

Spiteful gossips had caused speculation, controversy, and spread a most unfair rumour that the child, which had been born to Maria Beatrice of Modena, his Queen, had been smuggled into the Royal Bedchamber in a warming-pan.

This was entirely false, although the Prince had been premature at birth.

King Charles II's widow, the Dowager Queen Catherine, was present at the birth, as was Lord and Lady Sunderland and the Duchess of Portsmouth.

After the King's Declaration, the baby was created Prince of Wales at the age of four months. He was, however, unfortunate in that he was never crowned King.

October 24th   1851

A wild elopement

H.R.H. Prince Alexander was living in Russia where as Godson of the Tzar he had become a Major General in the Russian Imperial Army.

He was a brilliant, dashing and an extremely brave soldier and had received numerous decorations from the Tzar for his courage.

Back at Court after a victorious battle he fell in love.

His sister was married to the Tzarevitch and among her Ladies-in-Waiting was a very pretty Polish girl, Julie, Countess of Hauke.

Her father had been a general and Minister of War in Poland, but they were not noble.

In 1851 the Tzar told Alexander that he was to have the honour of marrying his niece, the Grand Duchess Catherine Michailova.

The Prince was horrified and because he was madly in love, he and Julie eloped.

They were married at Breslau on the 28th October by a nervous Priest.

The Tzar was furious, but fortunately the Prince's brother was now the Grand Duke Louis III and reigned in Hesse-Darmstadt.

He declared that the marriage was morganatic, but he would find a name for Julie.

He discovered there was a small village in the mountains called Battenburg.

Seven years later when the Countess of Battenburgh had given Prince Alexander several good-looking sons and a beautiful daughter, she became Her Serene Highness the Princess of Battenburg, and her children had the same rank.

Although none of them were aware of it, this was the beginning of the great and glorious family of Battenburg and Mountbatten.

October 25th   1920

A monkey bite

H.R.H. King Alexander had a dynamic career because he fell madly in love with Aspasia Manos, the daughter of an Aide-de-Camp of his father King Constantine.

She was extremely beautiful with a profile like one of the nymphs in a Classical Greek frieze. King Alexander had known her since they were children.

One night in November 1919 a Priest in the poorer quarter of Athens was woken by a loud knocking on his door.

He was told he was needed urgently and was driven to a private house. As soon as he arrived King Alexander and Aspasia asked the Priest to marry them.

There was consternation when the secret was discovered as the King had married without the consent of his father and the Head of the Church.

What was more, the populace were furious, and determined not to have a commoner on the Throne.

Finally, it was decided that 'Madame Manos' as she was called, should have no rank or title, but her daughter should be given the title of H.R.H. Princess Alexandra of Greece.

Despite so much difficulty Alexander and Aspasia were very happy. He died in 1920 from blood poison following a monkey bite.

October 26th   1612

A cordial from the Tower

The Prince of Wales, son of King James I, was ill for twelve days and every remedy known at the time was applied without success.

Finally, the Queen sent to the Tower of London for Sir Walter Raleigh's cordial. He had concocted it in a Laboratory he had been allowed to fit up in the Tower during his twelve-year imprisonment there.

Only fragments of his original formula remain, but it consisted of some forty roots, seeds, herbs and spices which Sir Walter may have brought back with him from South America.

Distilled in wine and combined with a mixture of red coral, dissolved pearls, hartshorn, musk and sugar, it was, someone said at the time, "a Witch's Brew!"

Unfortunately, the remedy gave Prince Henry only a slight relief from his pains, and finally on 6th November, he died.

October 27th   1868

Dolls on a honeymoon

H.R.H. Prince William of Glucksburg was elected to the Throne of Greece as King George I in 1863.

He took his position very seriously and confided to one of his companions that he was determined to be married as soon as it was possible.

Five years later he had an invitation from the Tzar of Russia to seek a wife.

The most suitable was the Grand Duchess Vera, daughter of the Tzar's youngest brother, The Grand Duke Constantine.

King William arrived at the Grand Duke's Palace and happened to look up in the hall. Looking down at him he saw a very shy, fair-haired lovely young girl.

It was the Duchess Olga, and it was love at first sight for both of them.

They were married in the Winter Palace and when they left for Greece the newly-wed Queen of the Hellenes, who was not yet sixteen, took her dolls with her.

October 28th   1931

A long wait

H.M. King George V and Queen Mary attend Noel Coward's pariotic new Musical, 'Cavalcade', at the Theatre Royal, Drury Lane.

During the second interval the brilliant young Author was presented to the King, and a rumour flashed round the auditorium that he had been knighted, there and then, in the Royal Box.

This only came true thirty-nine years later.

October 29th   1618

Sir Walter Raleigh beheaded

From being the favourite of H.M. Queen Elizabeth, Sir Walter's fortunes took a dramatic turn for the worse with the arrival of King James I.

He was imprisoned in the Tower for many years, but won the friendship of Prince Henry who could never understand how his father could keep 'so fine a bird in a cage.'

Eventually he was accused of being implicated in a conspiracy against the Monarch and sentenced to death.

October 30th   1651

A King on the run

The Royalist Forces were defeated at Worcester after which the future Charles II fled abroad after having wandered about England for forty-three days, living mostly on sherry and biscuits.

He darkened his face with walnut juice, had his hair cut with a pair of shears and donned green breeches, a leather doublet and a felt hat. He even imitated a country accent.

Charles's first refuge was at a house named 'Boscobel', north of Worcester, where he spent a day hiding in an oak tree, consuming large quantities of bread, cheese and beer.

He prayed he would escape detection from the pursuing Roundheads.

A reward of £1,000 was offered for his recapture – 'Charles Stuart, a long dark man, above two yards high' read the Parliamentary 'WANTED' notices.'

When his horse shed a shoe the Blacksmith remarked:

"If that rogue be taken he deserves to be hanged more than all the rest for bringing in the Scots!"

October 31st   1765

Too late

H.R.H. William, Duke of Cumberland was playing Piquet with General Hodson. He grew confused and mistook the cards.

The next day he recovered enough to appear at Court, but after dinner was seized with a suffocation and ordered the windows to be opened.

One of his valets, who was accustomed to bleed him was called and prepared to tie up his arm, but the Duke said:

"It is too late – it is all over!"

Then he died.

NOVEMBER

November 1st 965

A King wins

When H.M. King Edgar's first wife, Queen Ethelfleda, died he began to think about marrying again. He hoped to have more sons and so secure the succession.

Earl Athelwode was sent to visit Earl Ordgar to see if his daughter, the Lady Elfrida, lived up to her reputation of beauty and would make a suitable bride for the King. Athelwode himself fell in love with Elfrida and married her, telling the King that she was terribly ugly and would have made a deplorable Queen.

Months later, when King Edgar saw Elfrida, he realised that Athelwode had deceived him for she was the fairest women he had ever set eyes on.

He pretended not to be angry but suggested that he and Athelwode went hunting. In the midst of Harewood Forest King Edgar murdered Athelwode and on this day took the lovely widow as his Queen.

November 2nd   1717

A family tangle

H.R.H. The Princess of Wales, later to be Queen Caroline, gave birth to a son, William Augustus. It was hoped that this event might aid a reconciliation between King George I and the Prince of Wales since the baby's father asked the grandfather to stand sponsor.

Another godfather was to be George Augustus's uncle Ernest Augustus, Duke of York, but at the last minute the perverse King insisted that the Lord Chamberlain, the Duke of Newcastle, should take his place.

The Prince had long despised and hated Newcastle as incompetent and corrupt, and throughout the baptismal ceremony he fumed with anger. As the King departed, George Augustus could restrain himself no longer, walking up to the Duke and declaring:

"Rascal, I find you out!"

Unfortunately an extra element of drama was introduced by the Prince's bad pronunciation of English. Newcastle thought that the Prince had said 'fight' not 'find'.

Appalled, he hastened to the King, under the impression that he had been challenged to a duel by the heir to the throne. Though George later explained the mistake, he did so without concession of an apology. The King ordered his son's arrest.

When the Royal Ministers refused to have the Prince of Wales sent to the Tower, King George I resorted to ordering his son to leave the Palace immediately.

November 3rd   1600

A damnable beauty

H.M. King Henry IV of France had fallen under the spell of Henriette d'Entragues, a twenty-year-old brunette 'beautiful enough to bring damnation to men'.

She had managed to obtain from him a written promise of marriage and had given birth to a son who lived only a few hours.

Considering himself freed from his promise of marriage to her, the King prepared to meet his new wife Maria de Medici, who landed at Marseilles on November 3rd 1600. However, Henriette, who had followed the King, refused to leave him.

Making the excuse that he was already married to Maria by proxy, the King took the new Queen to bed immediately, to Henriette's raging fury.

November 4th   1834

The Princess to the rescue

H.R.H. Princess Victoria, with her mother, Lehzen and the Conroys, visited St Leonards-on-Sea. There occurred one of those accidents so common in the days of the horse.

The fifteen-year-old Princess took command like a true soldier's daughter in the moment of crisis. With the carriage overturned and two kicking horses on the ground, she first called for her dog to be rescued from the rumble and then 'ran on with him in my arms calling Mama to follow us'.

Princess Victoria ordered her party to take cover behind a well when one of the horses chased them down the road.

She created Mr Peckham Micklethwaite of Iridge, Sussex, a baronet in her Coronation Honours for having sat on its head.

November 5th   1605

The Gunpowder Plot

The Gunpowder Plot to blow up the English Parliament was originated by Robert Catesby, a strong leader of men and zealous Catholic idealist. He was deeply angry at the failure of King James I to improve the position of the Catholics in England as he had promised.

In May 1604 with a small group of relatives and friends, Catesby hired a house adjoining Parliament and dug a passage from the cellar to a point under the House of Lords.

In March 1605 they managed to rent the cellar next door, directly under the Palace of Westminster, and joined the two cellars by a passage.

Led by Guy Fawkes, a brave Yorkshire gentleman, a fanatical convert to the Catholic Church and Captain in the Spanish Army in the Netherlands, they stored about 20 barrels of gunpowder. Guy Fawkes looked after these under the name of John Johnson.

Due to unreliable men being told of the plot the secret came out and the King was warned. Guy Fawkes and the gunpowder plot were discovered due to cautionary searches before the opening of Parliament.

He was executed the following January with seven other conspirators.

November 6th   1785

A Royal conscience

H.R.H. Prince William wrote to his father to ask for the command of the 'Phaeton':

"I wish to be promoted, I do most anxiously; every officer does the same."

King George refused the request and inevitably the Prince solaced his desolation by falling in love with the young and very attractive Sarah Martin. A few months later he wrote:

"Do not imagine that I debauched the girl. Such a thought did not enter my head. The highest crime under Heaven next to murder is that of debauching innocent women; and is a crime I can with a safe conscience declare I never committed."

November 7th   1501

An impatient King

Princess Katharine of Aragon arrives in England to be married to H.R.H. Prince Arthur, Prince of Wales.

When King Henry VII heard the news he decided to forego the formal reception and ride out to meet his prospective daughter-in-law.

Katharine's Spanish retinue were horrified by this breach in etiquette and urged the King to wait until the wedding day. They told him that the Princess was resting.

"Tell the Lords of Spain," thundered Henry, "that the King will see the Princess even were she in her bed."

When Katharine appeared Henry was delighted by her clear complexion, auburn hair and well-formed figure.

November 8th   1852

A clever disguise

When Louis-Napoleon landed with 56 followers near to Boulogne, in an attempt to claim the French throne he was arrested, brought to trial and sentenced to permanent confinement. He spent six years in the fortress of Ham on the Somme marshes, writing pamphlets on sugar-beet and pauperism whilst studying to fit himself for his imperial role.

One day (May 25th 1846), taking matters into his own hands, since only the Government of Nicaragua had applied for his release, he shaved his beard and whiskers, donned a black wig and put on workman's trousers. Wearing four-inch wooden clogs to make him taller, he lifted a plank on to his shoulder and made for the gate.

As he approached the sentry, the white clay pipe drooping from his mouth fell to the ground. He picked up the pieces, continued on and arrived in London on Derby Day. He was made Emperor Napoleon III of France in November 1852.

November 9th   1740

A cruel ruler

Today the Empress Anna of Russia had a fit. She had been a cruel Ruler and was hated by the people. She had a passion for dwarfs and jesters. If a member of her Court offended she punished them by making them ape the antics of animals.

One had to sit in a specially constructed basket and cackle like a hen, for hours at a time, while another was made to go on all fours braying like a donkey.

A worse punishment for a Prince was because he married a Roman Catholic and became one himself. The Empress waited. When his first wife died she forced him to marry a hideous woman name Anna Buzheninova.

She then ordered the Governors of every part of the Nation to send to the capital a barbarous native of their Province to take part in their marriage.

The Bride and Bridegroom drove in a cage on the top of an elephant. When the Reception was over they were stripped naked and compelled to spend a night in a room where all the furniture was made of ice.

November 10th   1518

First words

As a child, Mary Tudor was very advanced for her age. When she was two, H.M. King Henry VIII carried her before an assembly of Courtiers.

Dutifully they kissed the baby's foot but she took no notice of them, looking about her until she caught sight of a Friar, who was the Royal organist.

To everyone's surprise she shouted out her first words, "Priest, priest!" and beckoned him to come and play for her.

This episode was later seen as an omen.

November 11th   1911

A Royal voyage to India

1911 was to be the first time that a reigning Sovereign had attended an Indian Durbar. It was to prove the last, so H.M. King George V and Queen Mary occupy a unique place in history.

They left of 11 November in the brand new P & O liner 'Medina'. Designed to carry six hundred and fifty passengers, she was occupied solely by the Royal party, which numbered twenty-four.

Queen Mary was delighted to be in India again. King George wrote in his diary of, 'the most wonderful Durbar ever held.'

One of Queen Mary's hosts fixed up a minor tiger-shoot for her. She climbed into a tree-hut and spotted a bear and some wild boars. She began knitting. Suddenly she pointed one of her needles towards the jungle and said to Lord Shaftesbury, who was in attendance:

"Look, Lord Shaftesbury, a tiger."

She said it very softly but the tiger disappeared before anyone could get a shot at it.

The Queen, probably relieved, went on knitting.

November 12th   1835

Russia has two Emperors

The Times of London reported on November 12th that "The Russian Empire is in the strange position of having two self-denying Emperors and no active Ruler."

The situation was unprecedented in the history of a Nation. The throne remained empty for three weeks after the death of Tzar Alexander I while his brother the Grand Duke Constantine and the Grand Duke Nicolas each wanted the other to wear the crown.

Duke Constantine refused but Grand Duke Nicolas was very unpopular. A riot outside the Palace ended in the death of sixty people. A conspiracy at which the Russians attempted to assassinate the Grand Duke was discovered.

Five leaders were condemned to death. Two hundred and eighty others were sent to Siberia for life.

Tzar Nicolas held a religious service on the day of the execution and in the evening Prince Kupucky gave a ball.

As the guests arrived bells were ringing and they saw a procession of carts filled with the friends and relations of the victims starting the long trek to Siberia.

The Princely exiles were accompanied by their wives, and in a gesture of defiance they wore evening dress, which their husbands were wearing when they were arrested.

As they passed the Palace the lights from the ballroom illuminated their ribbons and jewels, their pale and brave faces.

They were to be immortalised in the poems of Nekrasov and Pushkin.

November 13th   1794

Brave and fierce

H.R.H. Ernest Augustus, Duke of Cumberland, the fifth son of H.M. King George III, was both brave and very fierce.

One day, while fighting with a French Dragoon, he broke his

sabre, parried his adversary's blow with the stump, and, while the Frenchman was getting ready to strike again, calmly lifted him from the saddle and carried him off to the English lines.

The Frenchman, who had been encouraged by his Government to believe that all Princes were decadent, was no doubt too surprised to offer any resistance.

November 14th   1948

An Heir to the Throne is Born

H.R.H. Princess Elizabeth was expecting her first baby at any moment and a great crowd gathered outside the gates of Buckingham Palace to await the news.

Soon after nine in the evening a Police Inspector cupped his hands and turned to the crowd. "It's a Prince!"

The crowd outside the gates began singing and dancing for hours.

Although their loyal enthusiasm was appreciated by the Princess, it prevented her from sleeping.

When a message to this effect appeared on the notice board the crowd quietly dispersed.

November 15th   1191

Beautiful and good

Berengaria of Navarre was said to be the most beautiful woman of her generation. In 1191 she married King Richard I and became Queen of England, a country she was never to see.

Faithfully she waited in Aquitaine through the years of her husband's crusading and helped raise the ransom money while he was imprisoned.

Yet he did not send for his bride after his release and it was only when he fell ill and thought he was about to die that he eventually asked for her to join him.

He begged Berengaria to forgive his failings and vowed that he would never forsake her again. Nevertheless, King Richard's preference for members of his own sex meant that the marriage was never consummated.

When her husband died Berengaria was still young and beautiful and had been left great riches, but she never remarried and instead joined a Convent.

She spent the rest of her days feeding beggars and caring for abandoned children, and she financed the building of a stately Abbey at L'Epau.

November 16th   1734

Wanted – a husband

H.M. King George II's daughter, H.R.H. the Princess Anne, Princess Royal was convinced that she would make a great Queen if given the chance.

When she was sixteen years old there came a proposal from France that she should marry King Louis XV but religious prohibitions came between the Princess and her King.

In 1734 she married William, Prince of Orange – she would have taken any reasonable offer by them, to leave home and rule her own establishment.

The fact that the bridegroom was deformed and ugly did not deter her: she would have married a baboon, she told her father, rather than remain an Old Maid.

November 17th   1906

A rude awakening

H.M. The Emperor of Austria, Franz Joseph, was an excellent shot and enjoyed coming to England during the shooting season.

He stayed with the Duke of Devonshire at Chatsworth and a huge party was invited to meet him.

Chatsworth is an enormous building, yet despite its size the house was filled to overflowing with guests.

A friend who arrived late for the party was obliged to accept the Hall Porter's room as his bedroom. He was quite comfortable, but rather amazed the next morning when a number of letter bags were hurled on top of him and the postman shouted:

"Get up you lazy young devil! You've overslept yourself again!"

November 18th   1851

A disagreeable Royal

In 1837 H.R.H. Ernest Augustus, Duke of Cumberland, became King of Hanover.

One day a middle-aged lady appeared at his Court dressed in virgin white. The King deliberately pretended, with his bad sight, to mistake her for the fireplace which was painted white, and strolled up and started warming his back against her.

Until the day he died he used to tie yards of cravat round his neck to prevent his head from falling forward and to preserve the appearance of youth.

There is no denying that he was a highly disagreeable character, as King William IV summed him up:

"If anyone has a corn Ernest is sure to tread on it".

November 19th   1737

H.M. Queen Caroline dies

The day before she died, on her deathbed, Queen Caroline begged her husband to marry again. He sobbed:

"No, No, I shall have mistresses."

One of these was the outrageous Elizabeth Chudleigh.

She appeared at a Court masquerade as Iphigenia wearing only a thin robe of flesh-coloured silk which hid very little of her real flesh and everyone gasped.

The quick-witted Augusta, Princess of Wales, threw her veil over the girl, but not quickly enough to prevent the whole Court having an impression of complete nudity.

November 20th   1947

A happy wedding

H.R.H. Princess Elizabeth married Lieutenant Philip Mountbatten R.N. at Westminster Abbey.

On the previous day Prince Philip had been granted Royal status and on the actual day of his marriage the King made him Baron Greenwich, Earl of Merioneth and Duke of Edinburgh, and a Knight of the Garter.

The Bride's dress was designed by Norman Hartnell. It was of pearl-coloured satin embroidered in crystals and pearls, with a heart-shaped neckline and long, tight sleeves. The wedding ring was made from the same gold nugget from which the Queen's ring was made, mined in the Welsh hills.

Princess Elizabeth's favourite hymn, 'Praise, my soul, the King of Heaven' was chosen for the opening processional hymn.

They were both very much in love, and went for their Honeymoon to Broadlands, the home of Lord Mountbatten in Romsey.

November 21st

Five at a time

Kubla Khan, Emperor of China, had an enormous harem of concubines who were chosen for him with the greatest care by a number of people he appointed as professionals at the job.

After approximately two years, the fortunate girls to be chosen from over 200 at a time, would share the Emperor's bed in batches of five at a time.

The Emperor fathered 47 sons and innumerable daughters who had not been counted.

This unusual and what might be thought exhausting physical enjoyment did not in any way damage his health.

In fact, the great Khan lived to the age of 79 which was exceedingly remarkable in the 13th century.

November 22nd   1939

Under the influence

The bearded Artist, Augustus John, had accepted a commission to paint the Queen. A preliminary meeting was arranged to take place on this day, at which John failed to turn up.

He sent a strange telegram to Buckingham Palace saying he was suffering from 'the influence'.

Sittings began shortly afterwards and bottles of sherry and brandy were placed in a cupboard by the Palace staff to help the great Artist with his work.

When he was lent a home in the South of France by Sir James Dunn, it took several days to remove the mountain of empty bottles which had accumulated in the back of the garden.

November 23rd   1865

A capital profit

The Emperor Napoleon called his mistress, 'La Castiglione' –
'The Queen of Hearts'. She was very beautiful, but not as witty as
some of the other dozen Courtesans, known as 'La Garde'. They
were queens of their profession. Each of these women considered
her beauty was her capital and made it pay breath-taking dividends.

"When I have been to your house," said Alphonse de Rothschild,
the enormously rich banker, to one of the Grand Cocottes, "It
makes mine seem like a hovel!"

November 24th   1793

A Prince in trouble

H.R.H. Prince Augustus the sixth son of H.M. King George III
had fallen madly in love with Lady Augusta Murray. He was
nineteen and she was thirty.

A handsome young man who suffered with 'convulsive asthma'
he could not serve in the Army like his brothers. Instead he was a
classical scholar and owned 5000 Bibles.

He was aware that his marriage with Lady Augusta must be kept
secret, and he found a Clergyman called Gunn to marry them.

He wrote to Lady Augusta:
"If Gunn will not marry me, I shall die."
Gunn did marry them at St. George's Hanover Square on the

24th November 1793, and a year later in January Augusta gave birth to a son at her parent's home.

The same month the King learned of the marriage. He was furious. He kept the Prince abroad and forbade his wife to join him. They did not see each other for six years.

But finally they found happiness until she died.

November 25th   1906

A successful battle

H.M. Alfonso XIII of Spain astonished everyone by winning the clay-pigeon trophy in the Isle of Wight.

Earlier in the year he had survived an assassination attempt on his Wedding Day.

He was in fact a very good shot and became extremely impressed by the driven sport which he saw at Windsor Castle when he was staying with the King and Queen.

So much so, that he was determined to copy it. He hired an Englishman to come out to his Private Estate at Casa de Campo and to bring with him 2,000 pheasants' eggs and some red legged partridge.

The Englishman whose name was Watts, organised a *battue* in the English style which was a huge success.

November 26th   1609

Crowned by death

On this day Princess H.R.H. Henrietta Maria was born at the Louvre. After the birth Henrietta's mother, Marie de Medici, begged her husband, King Henry IV of France, to allow her to be crowned.

The King himself had been crowned some years before his marriage but had postponed the Queen's official enthronement year after year. This was because he was still mindful that a soothsayer had told him that he would die the day after his wife's coronation. However, he eventually agreed that the ceremony should take place.

Marie de Medici was crowned on May 10th 1610, and the day after the King returned to Paris from St Denis. As his coach rumbled over the cobble-stones into the busy Rue de la Ferronerie, it was forced to slow owing to the press of the traffic. At that moment a bystander leapt on to a spoke of one of the great carriage wheels, leaned through the window, and plunged a knife into Henry's heart.

The assassin was Francois Ravaillac, a teacher who suffered from religious mania, and believed that King Henry was going to make war on the Pope.

November 27th   1965

'A schoolboy's triumph'

H.R.H. the Prince Charles was to crown his last year at
Gordonstoun in a field in which his father never shone:– the school
play at Christmas.

The Prince was cast in the role of Shakespeare's Macbeth. Thirty
years earlier, Prince Philip had qualified only for that of Lord
Donalbain, an attendant.

A fortnight after their son's seventeenth birthday, The Queen
and Prince Philip flew north to see him strut the stage in front of
Gordonstoun's version of Glamis Castle, ancestral home of his
Grandmother's family – the Bowes-Lyons.

The Prince looked so convincing that the Gordonstoun thes-
pians were accused of importing professional make-up artists. It was
not true, the Royal chin experienced the familiar schoolboy agonies
of tufts of crepe hair stuck on with glue.

Prince Charles was a triumph and the *Gordonstoun Record*
reported:

"He was at his very best in the quiet poetic soliloquies, and in the
bits which expressed Macbeth's terrible agony of remorse and fear."

November 28th   1561

The Nut Girl

One of H.M. Queen Elizabeth's suitors was H.R.H. Prince Eric
of Sweden. He had sent his brother to plead his cause, and
Elizabeth playfully raised his hopes by sending the artist Van der

September 20th 1936

H.M. King Edward VIII had fallen in love with Mrs Wallis Simpson and
he dismissed Mrs Dudley Ward, his Mistress of many years. When she
tried to telephone him she was unable to speak with him.

October 23rd 1688

H.M. King James II was obliged to make a Declaration that the birth of his son James Francis Edward had been witnessed. Spiteful gossips had spread the rumour that the child had been smuggled into the Royal bedchamber in a warming-pan.

October 30th 1651

H.M. Charles II became associated with the oak tree after the Battle of Worcester. Defeated by Roundheads, he hid for a day under a large oak, consuming large quantities of bread, cheese and beer.

November 5th 1605

H.M. James I provoked the wrath of Rober Catesby, a strong leader of men, who organized the gunpowder plot to blow up Parliament with 20 barrels of gunpowder. The secret was revealed and the King was warned. The conspirators were executed.

November 29th 1289

H.M. Queen Eleanor died of a fever and her husband H.M. King Edward I was devastated, as they loved each other passionately. King Edward's words of grief still move us. 'My harp is turning to mourning. In life I loved her dearly, how can I cease to love her in death.'

December 7th 1662

H.M. Charles II was frustrated in his attempts to conquer 'La Belle Stuart', most beautiful of Queen Catherine's maids-of-honour. The monarch despaired when she finally married the Duke of Richmond, and wrote a poem about his jealousy.

December 10th 1542

In old age H.M. King Henry VIII was increasingly vindictive. He had discovered that his fifth wife, Catherine Howard has been repeatedly unfaithful. On this day she, together with her lover, was executed.

December 16th 1685

H.M. Queen Mary of Modena wife of King James II, was initially infuriated by the presence of her husband's mistress, Catherine Sedley, at Court. But during her absence the Queen realised that she was more beautiful than her rival, and decided to ignore her.

Meulen to paint his portrait. The painting failed to impress her and she rejected Prince Eric.

Prince Eric consoled himself by marrying one of his most humble subjects, Kate the Nut Girl. Astonished by her beauty when he saw her selling nuts in the square before his palace, he fell in love with her and when he found her 'virtue impregnable', he made her his Queen.

It was one of the most successful Royal marriages in Europe, and she remained a model of love and loyalty even when Eric was supplanted by his brother John who finally murdered him.

November 29th   1289

Crosses where a Queen rested

H.M. Queen Eleanor died of a fever today and her husband H.M. King Edward I was devastated as they loved each other passionately.

As the enormous funeral procession moved South with the embalmed body, everywhere they stopped for the night the King had a Cross erected, so he said:

"That passengers reminded might pray for her soul."

Today out of the twelve crosses the King commanded nine have vanished. Only three remain at Waltham, Northampton and Geddington.

The site of the original cross at the top of Whitehall is usurped by the statue of King Charles I.

Yet King Edward's words of grief still move us.

"My harp is turning to mourning. In life I loved her dearly, how can I cease to love her in death."

30th November   1936

The burning of the Crystal Palace

H.M. Queen Mary decided that an air of calm must be induced, to scotch any rumours which might be flying around about King Edward VIII's possible abdication.

To this end she appeared in public as much as possible visiting Exhibitions, the London Museum, and going to the big Stores to buy Christmas presents.

The people of South London saw her when the Crystal Palace on Sydenham Hill burned down. For her it was a symbolic tragedy.

It buried the outstanding memory of Prince Albert the Consort, at the moment when the foundations of the British throne were shaking.

DECEMBER

December 1st   1924

80th birthday

H.M. The Queen Mother Queen Alexandra celebrated her 80th birthday. She was a great beauty when she arrived in England in 1863; she was still beautiful, but inevitably disliked the obvious traces of age.

She wrote to an old friend:

"Now I am breaking up, think of me as I used to be."

She was completely deaf and her eyesight was growing worse. When she died in November 1925, four Kings walked behind her coffin and seventeen British and Foreign Princesses.

For the first time the King's Principal Flying A.D.C. was with those of the Army and Navy.

December 2nd   1674

A Court Masque

Court Masques, which had been very popular in King James I's reign and encouraged by his wife, Anne of Denmark, were revived for a brief time in England during the Restoration of the Monarchy in the 1660's.

However, with the advent of professional actresses to the Theatre and a new vogue for professional drama, amateur theatricals at Court lost favour.

One of the last notable Masques was '*Calisto or the Chaste Nymph*' by Crowne which was performed on this day. Two future Queens, H.R.H. Princess Mary and Princess Anne of York took part: they had been coached in their roles by the fashionable actress Mrs Betterton.

Another performer, impersonating goddess Diana, was Margaret Blagge, the Duchess of York's former Maid of Honour. She was very reluctant to take part, being extremely devout and felt unsure of the efficacy of flaunting her talents on the stage.

To make matters worse, on the night ot the performance, she lost a diamond worth £80 which she had borrowed from the Countess of Suffolk.

December 3rd   1891

The Duke of Clarence

H.R.H. Prince Eddy was encouraged to marry due to the scandal his private life had been causing. H.M. Queen Victoria considered Princess May of Teck was:

"A particularly nice girl, so quiet and yet cheerful and so very carefully brought up and so sensible. She is grown very pretty."

The Prince was urged to propose and this he did at Luton Hoo. He was dancing with Princess May. The strains of the Blue Danube lifted the feet of the dancing couples, the heat and the scent of flowers went to his head. Rumours may have reached her that something was afoot; everyone was complimenting her on her gown.

Prince Eddy took the Princess by the hand and led her into the Boudoir. There he proposed to her. She said afterwards:

"To my great surprise Eddy proposed to me . . . . Of course I said Yes! We are both very happy. Kept it secret from everybody but Mama and Papa."

The marriage never took place. Albert Victor died of pneumonia in January 1892 and Princess May married his younger brother, George who became King George V.

December 4th   1785

A kind King

One day whilst out walking during this bitter winter, H.M. King George III was approached by two sorrowful little boys.

They did not realise that it was the King and begged him for food, telling between their sobs of how their mother had just died and that their father lay gravely ill.

The King insisted on accompanying the boys home and discovered the father desperately clinging to the body of their dead mother.

The Monarch took great pity on the family and as well as providing them with their immediate needs he offered to provide for the boys' future and education.

December 5th   1560

Death of H.M. King Francis II of France

The beautiful red-haired Mary Stuart had been sent as a Catholic to be educated at the Court of France in August 1558. She married H.M. King Francis the same year.

He was feeble in spirit and suffered constantly from the most atrocious headaches, and probably had tuberculosis.

This illness tends to excite sexual appetites, and there is no doubt that the lovely new Queen was also very sensual. They had a frenzied, passionate relationship which overwhelmed the King and hastened his death.

Queen Mary was no longer welcome in the France of Queen Catherine de Medici. She left France for Scotland to meet her tragic destiny.

December 6th   1789

Daughter of a cook is guillotined

Jeanne was the love-child of Anne Becu, a cook in a small village in Champagne. Beautiful, fair-haired and wildly seductive, she was ambitious enough at the age of sixteen to live with the Comte du Barry.

He was a loathsome man who hired her out to any man who paid for her but through him she was taken to the old, tired, disillusioned King Louis XV. He became infatuated with her.

To legalise her position she was married to the Comte du Barry's brother after which she was presented at Court on January 25th 1769.

King Louis XV contracted smallpox. Jeanne was the only person who tended him. The new King and his Queen – Marie Antoinette – were soon facing a Revolution.

Jeanne took several more lovers – the last being the Duc de Brissac. He was guillotioned and Jeanne was arrested.

A daughter of the people, she was accused of being an aristocrat and was taken to *Le Place de la Revolution*.

"Just one more moment of life," she pleaded, as the grey blade began its descent.

As her head fell into the basket, her perfect lips which had known so many kisses, formed the words:
"Vie – Vie – Vie!"

December 7th   1662

A King's hell

H.M. King Charles II was unhappy and frustrated. He had fallen in love with the most beautiful of Queen Catherine's maids-of-honour known as *La Belle Stuart'*.

The King lusted after Frances and became miserable with jealousy when she refused him.

Frances's favourite pastimes at Court were 'Blind Man's Buff', 'Hunt the Slipper' and building houses out of playing cards.

But she would not agree to climb into bed with the King.

The Monarch finally despaired when she eventually married the Duke of Richmond and the King wrote a pathetic poem about his jealousy.

"While alone to myself I repeat all her charms,
She I love may be locked in another man's arms,
She may laugh at my cares and so false she may be,
To say all the kind things she before said to me;
O then, 'tis O then, that I think there's no hell
Like loving too well."

December 8th   1907

A Royal rebuke

H.M. King Edward VII was very quick to rebuke anyone who he thought was not behaving with propriety.

He told off the Duchess of Marlborough when she appeared at dinner without a tiara.

"The Queen", he said severely, "wears a tiara. Why not you?"

On another occasion an Admiral's daughter forgot the time and arrived at a Royal party in a dress which was an inch above her ankles.

"I am afraid you must have made a mistake", the King said tartly, "this is a dinner, not a tennis party."

December 9th   1706

The art of love

H.M. King Pedro's son, King Joao V was a larger than life
Monarch of the Baroque period.

There was a certain resemblance between him and his contem-
porary, Augustus "The Strong" of Saxony.

He was an art lover and his taste was impeccable. It was said of
him that "his love of God equalled his love of women" and he raised
"a chain of costly Churches and a multitude of natural children".

Owing to the large sums of money which he lent to the Papacy,
Pope Benedict XIV conferred on him the title of "Most Faithful
Majesty".

December 10th   1542

Lovers pay the price

In November H.M. King Henry VIII discovered that his fifth
wife, Catherine Howard, had been repeatedly unfaithful to him.
She had carried on her intrigues right under his nose.

Queen Catherine had flirted with one of her husband's closest
intimates, Thomas Culpepper, and more than likely seduced him.

She was clearly the aggressor, not the victim, and in her blind
desperation she failed to conceal her passion from her Bedchamber
woman, who now testified against her. There could be no leniency
for someone who had cuckolded the King.

On December 10th Culpepper was executed together with
another of Catherine's lovers, Francis Dereham.

December 11th   1936

The Abdication

Lady Cynthia Asquith had been invited to 145 Piccadilly this morning when the instrument of Abdication was ratified by Parliament and George VI became King.

Princess Elizabeth looked at a letter on the hall table which was addressed to 'Her Majesty, the Queen'.

"That's Mummy now, isn't it?" she asked Lady Cynthia.

The younger Princess, Margaret Rose, complained:

"I had only just learned how to spell York – Y–O–R–K – and now I am not to use it any more. I am to sign myself Margaret alone."

December 12th   1936

H.M. King George VI succeeds to the Throne

At his Accession Council in St. James's Palace he said:

"With my wife as helpmeet by My side, I take up the heavy task which lies before Me. In it I look for the support of all my peoples."

His first speech as King was delivered haltingly in a low, nervous voice.

In his diary he confessed that in talking to his mother Queen Mary about the Abdication he broke down and "sobbed like a child."

December 13th   1906

H.H. Princess Marina of Greece and Denmark is born in Athens

A gypsy woman foretold, shortly after her birth:
"She is a child of destiny and there is both sunshine and shadow for her. She will be beautiful and make a great marriage with a King's son.
Love will be her guiding star. It will bring her sorrow, for she will lose her husband while she is still young and at the height of her happiness. But she will find consolation in her children."

December 14th   1987

The Duchess of York wins her helicopter 'wings'

On this day the Duchess fulfilled the pledge made on the eve of her wedding when she said of Prince Andrew:
"Flying is his life and I want to be part of his life".
She became the first member of the Royal Family to hold a private helicopter licence. The Duke said:
"She's amazing, learning to fly a helicopter in just over 40 hours. It took me 85 hours to get my wings."

December 15th   1369

An evil tale

H.M. Queen Philippa, wife of King Edward III, was notable as being a most courteous, liberal and noble lady.

During her lifetime, there was never one word said about her except in praise and exaltation.

Then a few years after her death when the King had fallen into the clutches of a harpy named Alice Perrers, a strange story was whispered about the Palace.

It was that Queen Philippa's son, John of Gaunt, was not the son of King Edward as everyone believed.

It was said that Queen Philippa had borne a daughter and rather than disappoint her husband whom she loved, she had smuggled in a boy, son of a labouring man of Gaunt, and she had brought him up as her own.

Whoever invented the story which was supposed to have been confided on her death-bed to William of Wykeham, founder of Winchester College, and New College Oxford, did not however take family resemblances into account.

John of Gaunt was a typical Plantaganet. The wicked little story hung about and soured John's temper and made him a difficult person to live with.

Alice Perrers doubtless invented the story for her own means. As soon as King Edward ceased breathing in the Palace of Sheen near Richmond, she pulled the rings from his fingers and stole them for herself.

December 16th   1685

A persistent Mistress

H.M. King James II's consort, Mary of Modena, was infuriated by the presence of her husband's mistress, Catherine Sedley, at Court. One day she could contain her rage no longer and told him:

"Give her my dower, make her Queen of England, but let me never see her more!"

Catherine left London for a short while but soon returned and the King made her Countess of Dorchester. The Queen took to her bed and in the presence of her Catholic priests presented her husband with an ultimatum.

As he appeared to make her suffer such a degradation, and showed an utter disregard for the most sacred obligations, either he must give up his mistress, or she would withdraw to a Convent.

King James, taken by surprise at the Queen's tears and her Priest's remonstrations, promised to finish the disgraceful affair.

Catherine, however, refused to leave London declaring that she was a freeborn Englishwoman and would live where she pleased.

In the end King James bribed her with the present of an estate in Ireland. Nevertheless she returned after a few months but by this time Queen Mary had regained her composure. She realised that she was far more beautiful than her rival, and decided to ignore her.

December 17th   1833

The Queen and the Corporal

H.C.H. Maria Cristina the Queen Regent of Spain was twenty-six when her husband, King Fernando VIII whom she had nursed devotedly died in 1833.

She was very attractive and when she smiled, 'every man's heart was at her feet.'

As a Bourbon she had a passionate nature which had been suppressed when she was the fourth wife of a very old, ill man. One afternoon the Queen was with her Troops when her nose began to bleed.

She used up her own handkerchief and those of her Ladies-in-Waiting and they borrowed one from their escort.

When the Queen returned it she saw he was a dark, handsome, muscular, sensual looking man. With an unusual chivalry he raised the blood stained handkerchief to his lips. For months Corporal Munoz haunted the young Queen's dreams.

One day she was travelling across the snow-covered Guadarrame mountains escorted by two officers and Corporal Munoz.

There was an accident and again the Corporal offered his handkerchief.

Later the Queen started to walk with one of the Officers and the Corporal. Some distance from home she sent the Officer back for an umbrella. Alone with the man she loved, she told him of her feelings and proposed marriage.

Munoz, son of simple people who kept a tobacco shop, fell on his knees and burst into tears.

Within three months of widow-hood, the Queen and Munoz were married secretly and were wildly and ecstatically happy.

December 18th   1840

Perfect love

H.R.R. Prince George, eldest son of the Duke of Cambridge, went to a pantomime and promptly fell in love with Miss Louisa Fairbrother, who was playing the part of Columbine.

The Prince had always adored beautiful women, he was determined to marry Louisa believing that to marry for any other reason than love was shameful.

Realising that Queen Victoria would never consent to the match he married Louisa secretly in St John's Church, Clerkenwell.

Although the Prince was often away on military duty the couple exchanged many loving letters. Their marriage was never officially recognised but they enjoyed a faithful and adoring relationship until Louisa's death in 1890.

Her Royal husband wrote:

"My beloved one lay lovely in death still amongst us. Her countenance was beautiful, quite young to look at, although 74 in actual age . . . She was so good, kind, affectionate, true and generous-hearted. My little home of 50 years with my beloved Louisa is now come to an end."

December 19th   1888

Spinach upsets the King

Before he became H.M. King Edward VII, the Prince of Wales was sometimes known to display remarkable outbursts of temper.

One day he was at dinner at a country-house party and a footman splashed a little creamed spinach on his shirt front. The guests watched with horrified eyes while the Prince of Wales thrust his hand into the dish of spinach and, flaming with rage, rubbed a handful of spinach in circles all over his starched front.

He darted to his feet, muttering:

"May as well make a complete job of it!"

In the petrified hush he strode from the Dining-Room. He reappeared later in the evening in a perfectly unruffled mood.

December 20th   1670

The curtain falls

The Mistresses of Charles II were getting older and finding it harder to compete with their new and younger rivals. For the beautiful Barbara Castlemaine, high living, late hours and long drinking had begun to take its toll.

She was pensioned off on this day as the Duchess of Cleveland.

She was a relative of the King's Jester and poet, The Earl of Rochester. She had helped his marriage but he had noted all her infidelities against the King and had recorded them: Monmouth and Cavendish, Henningham and Scope 'Scabby Ned', and 'Sturdy Franch'.

He wrote in his usual cynical manner:

'When she has jaded quite,

Her almost boundless appetite . . .

She'll still drudge on in tasteless vice,

As if she sinn'd for exercise.'

December 21st   1785

A secret marriage

  H.R.H. The Prince of Wales (later George IV) and Mrs Maria Fitzherbert were secretly married by an Anglican Clergyman. The ceremony took place in her Drawing Room with his Uncle and younger brother present.

  Afterwards the Bride and Bridegroom left immediately for their honeymoon. Under Canon Law the marriage is valid but by the laws of the land it is invalid.

December 22nd   1525

Off his guard

  Cardinal Wolsey had built himself the most magnificent Palace ever seen at Hampton Court.

  Apart from the huge amazing building itself, throughout the Palace could be seen a profusion of gold and silver plate and ornaments, bowls and salt cellars encrusted with rubies, diamonds and pearls.

  The Venetian Ambassador calculated their actual worth to be three hundred thousand ducats, about five million pounds in today's money.

  In H.M. King Henry VIII's mind there slowly festered a certain jealousy of his Chief Minister's high living.

  Talking together in one of the splendid rooms he suddenly asked the Cardinal why he had built such a majestic home for himself.

The Cardinal, off his guard, made a fatal reply:

"To show how noble a Palace a subject may offer to his Sovereign."

Like the snappy jaws of a crocodile, King Henry instantly accepted the generous 'offer'.

Hampton Court and all its treasures were formally conveyed to the King.

Wolsey was allowed to remain in reisdence but only as a Royal 'tenant'.

December 23rd   A.D. 210

Steeplechasing

Today, the first Horse Race recorded in England took place at Wetherby, North Yorkshire.

The Emperor of Rome, Lucius Septimus Severus, brought Arabian horses to Britain which competed in it.

Steeplechases became popular all down the centuries. The Bucks and Beaux of the Regency made them dangerous by riding at night when they were drunk.

The Grand National Steeplechase which began in 1837 as the Grand Liverpool Steeplechase, has become the most famous and important steeplechase throughout the world.

The course must be covered twice, with a distance of 4 miles, 856 yards, and a total of 30 jumps.

December 24th   1913

Holy headache

Menelik II, Emperor of Ethiopia invented for himself a strange form of the Christian Religion.

If he felt ill, he would not call in doctors or have any of the known conventional medicines. Instead he would turn to the Bible.

However this was not for the spiritual comfort it might bring him but for the healing properties of the pages on which it was printed.

When he had an upset stomach, a cold or a headache, the Emperor would tear out a few pages and eat them and he told all his subjects that this remedy never failed.

On this day in December 1913 when he was recovering from a stroke and feeling exceedingly unwell, he decided that what he needed was a large amount of the medicine in which he believed.

He had the entire Book of Kings pulled out from the Old Testament and ate every page.

Unfortunately it proved to be an overdose and he died.

December 25th   1939

H.H. King George VI's first broadcast

His Majesty includes in his first Christmas Broadcast of the war a poem which was to become his epitaph.

It was a collection of poems called *The Desert*, written by Miss 'Minnie' (Marie Louise) Haskins, a Lecturer of the London School of Economics. It was entitled '*The Gate of the Year*'

"I said to the man who stood at the Gate of the Year,
'Give me a light so that I may tread safely into the unknown,'
And he replied: 'Go out into the darkness,
And put your hand into the Hand of God.
That shall be to you better than light,
And safer than a known way.'   —

December 26th   1913

Was it fate?

H.R.H. Franz Ferdinand of Austria stayed at Welbeck Abbey, the home of the Duke of Portland, in December 1913.

He was a very distinguished shot, but while he was there he had a very narrow escape. There was deep snow on the ground and during a drive one of the loaders fell down.

Both barrels of the gun he was holding went off and the shot passed within a few feet of the Archduke. He was unharmed and laughed it off.

But the following year his death in Sarajevo was the spark which ignited the First World War.

Those who remembered the incident at Welbeck Abbey wondered whether if it had not been a near-miss, history might have been changed, and millions of lives spared.

December 27th   1902

The missing Queen

H.M. Queen Alexandra organised a Christmas Dinner for 1,500 war widows and their families. She personally insisted upon supervising all the arrangements.

The puddings were to be piped in by the Scots Guards, there were to be presents for all and a full programme of famous variety artistes was prepared to enliven the proceedings.

Unfortunately, on the great day, Queen Alexandra lay in bed in deep distress with a violent cold, and the dinner she had looked forward to so eagerly had to take place without her.

December 28th   1700

The Dutch monster

H.M. King William III had such atrocious manners that even his sister-in-law, who became Queen Anne after his death, referred to him as the 'Dutch Monster'.

One of Princess Anne's ladies gives an example of his vulgar behaviour at his own table.

She writes:

"There happened to be a plate of peas; the first that had been seen that year. The King, without offering the Princess the least share of them, ate every one himself. Whether he offered any to the Queen I cannot say; but he might do safely enough for he knew she durst not touch them. The Princess confessed, when she came home, she wanted the peas so much that she was afraid to look at them, and yet could hardly keep her eyes off them."

The death of Queen Mary had such a profound effect on King William that he started to drink heavily. His body shrank to a pitiful thinness while his legs became very swollen.

His Physician, Dr Radcliffe, upon examining them said heartlessly:

"I would not have Your Majesty's legs for your three Kingdoms!"

December 29th   1364

A new fashion

H.M. King Richard II was very happy with his wife, Anne of Bohemia, who was very attractive.

Soon after she was married, when she was only eighteen, she introduced the side-saddle for riding horses. Until this time, English women who rode on horseback rode astride, the weight evenly balanced.

After Queen Anne's innovation with both the female rider's legs on one side, a lot of horses had sore backs and all the ladies rode in a cramped and precarious posture.

Gradually the fashion adjusted itself and became something very beautiful and outstanding which delighted artists as well as equestrians.

Queen Anne died in 1394 struck down by a plague. It was not connected with the Great Plague but just a summer plague in June at her favourite palace at Richmond.

King Richard was inconsolable and broken-hearted. In a rough and turbulent world she had been his true partner and his real love. She shared his taste for the more beautiful things in life.

An effigy of Anne of Bohemia lies beside that of her husband, King Richard II, in Westminster Abbey.

December 30th   1883

An amazing guest

Among the guests H.M. Queen Victoria entertained at Balmoral was Rudolf Slatin.

He had been born in 1857 of a well known Viennese family and was known as Pasha, a title given to him by the Khedive of Egypt.

He became a professional soldier and went to the Sudan to serve with the Egyptian Government under General Gordon's direction.

In 1881 he was appointed Governor-General of the Egyptian Province of Darfur. Two years later he became nominally a Muslim, believing that it was the only way to hold the loyalty of his troops against the rise of the fanatic religious escetic, the Mahdi.

In December 1883, he was forced to surrender to the Mahdi, and was held prisoner by him and his successor, the Khalifa, until February 1895, when he escaped to Cairo.

Queen Victoria wrote in her diary that she thought he was:

". . . . charming modest little man, whom no one could think had gone through such vicissitudes, for he looks so well. But there are lines in his face which betoken mental suffering. His final escape was quite miraculous. He had been eleven years in captivity and nine months in irons. While he was in prison they brought him General Gordon's head."

December 31st   1817

A Royal supper for the staff

H.R.H. The Prince Regent who was frequently in Brighton supervising the renovations that were being made to the Royal Pavilion, often visited the kitchens.

As a dedicated gourmet and gastronome, his food was of paramount importance and his French Chefs frequently served up dinners of thirty-six courses.

He decided as a Christmas present to his staff he would give them a party. A scarlet cloth was thrown over the kitchen floor, a splendid repast was provided, and His Royal Highness sat down with a select party of his friends.

The whole of the servants, especially the females, were delighted with the idea and the supper, His Royal Highness said afterwards, it was one of the most successful parties he had ever given, adding:

"At least the guests were extremely grateful for what they received."

ACKNOWLEDGEMENTS
BY BARBARA CARTLAND

I wish to thank Catherine Moriarty for her help in the very extensive research for this book.

Also two of my Secretaries, Mrs. Audrey Elliott who has collected a great many of the illustrations and Mrs. Hazel Clark who has helped to edit this book.

I am also very grateful to the Authors of the long list of books I have consulted. These I have not only used for this production, but their words are a joy and delight and an inspiration for every novel I write.

Charles Allen and Sharada Dwivedi, "Lives of the Indian Princes"; Archibald: "The Wooden Fighting Ship"; Sue Arnold, "Little Princes from Cradle to Crown"; Dulcie M. Ashdown, "Royal Children", "Royal Paramours", "Ladies-in-Waiting"; Maurice Ashley, "The Life and Times of William I"; Andrew Barrow, "Gossip. A History of High Society from 1920–1970"; John Barton and Joy Law, "The Hollow Crown"; Georgina Battiscombe, "Queen Alexandra", Bryan Bevan, "Charles the Second's French Mistress"; Madeleine Bingham, "Earls and Girls, Dramas?"; Jeffrey Finestone, "The Last Courts of Europe"; Antonia Fraser, "Charles II", "Mary Queen of Scots"; Roger Fulford, "Royal Dukes"; Mollie Gillen, "Royal Duke"; Graham Greene, "Lord Rochester's Monkey"; Prince Michael of Greece, "The Crown Jewels of Britain and Europe"; Evelyn Hall-King, "Passionate Lives"; Joseph Haslip, "Marie Antionette"; Oliver Hedley, "Queen Charlotte"; Christopher Hibbert, "The Court At Windsor. A Domestic History", "George IV Regent and King", "Queen Victoria in Her Letters and Journals"; Anthony Holden, "Charles Prince of Wales", "Their Royal High-nesses, The Prince and Princess of Wales"; Paul James, "The Royal Almanac"; Denis Judd, "Eclipse of Kings. European Monarchies in the Twentieth Century"; R Roll Lindsey, "Country Life Book of Europe's Royal Families"; Harold Kurtz, "The Empress Eugenie"; Richard Hough, "Advice to a Granddaughter"; Robert Lacey, "The Life and Times of Henry VIII"; Dorothy Laird, "Royal Ascot"; Pater Lane, "The Queen Mother"; The London Gazette; John Lord, "The Maharajahs"; Elizabeth Longford, "Queen Victoria R.I."; N.E. McClure, "The Letters of John Chamberlain"; Victor Mallet, "Life with Queen Victoria, 1887– 1901"; Dorothy Marshall, "Victoria"; Brian Masters, "The Mistress of Charles II"; Keith Middlemas, "The Life and Times of George VI"; Nancy Mitford, "The Sun King"; Patrick Morrah, "A Royal Family. Charles I and his Family"; Roy Nash, "Hampton Court"; J.E. Neale, "Queen Elizabeth"; D.D.R. Owen,

"Noble Lovers"; Tony Palmer, "Charles II. Portrait of an Age"; Sally Patience, "The Queen Mother"; Alison Plowden, "The Young Victoria", "The Young Elizabeth"; Frederick Ponsonby, "Recollections of Three Reigns"; James Pope-Hennessy, "Queen Mary"; J.B. Priestley, "The Prince of Pleasure and his Regency 1811–20"; David Randall, "Royal Follies"; Dr. Angelo S. Rappoport, "Mad Majesties or Raving Rulers and Sub-missive Subjects"; Michaela Reid, "Ask Sir James"; Joanna Richardson, "The Courtesans"; John Martin Robinson, "Royal Residences"; Gwen Robyns, "Geraldine of the Albanians"; Kenneth Rose, "Kings, Queens and Courtiers"; Jonathan Garnier Ruffer, "The Big Shots"; Desmond Seward, "The Bourbon Kings of France"; J.J. Scarisbrick, "Henry VIII"; Christopher Sinclair-Stevenson, "Blood Royal. The Illustrious House of Hanover"; A. Kenneth Snowman, "Carl Fabergé. Goldsmiths to The Imperial Court of Russia"; Godfrey Talbot, "The Country in High Society"; Olivia Bland, "The Royal Way of Death"; Wilfred Blunt, "The Dream King. Ludwig II of Bavaria"; Elizabeth Burton, "The Pageant of Early Tudor England"; Ethel Carleton Williams, "Anne of Den-mark"; Charles Carlton, "Charles I, The Personal Monarch"; Beatrice Fairbanks Cayzer, "The Princes and Princesses of Wales"; Chambers, "The Book of Days. A Miscellany of Popular Antiquities"; Brigadier Stanley Clark, O.B.E., "Palace Diary"; Virginia Cowles, "The Romanovs. The Last Tsar and Tsarina"; Lesley Cunliffe, "Great Royal Disasters"; Debratt's "Book of the Royal Wedding" (Prince Andrew and Sarah Ferguson); John Dent, "The Quest for Nonsuch"; E.G. Dickens, "The Courts of Europe, Politics, Patron-age and Royalty"; F. Dimond and K. Taylor, "Crown and Camera. The Royal Family and Photography. 1842–1910"; Julia Dobson, "Children of Charles I"; Hebe Dorsey, "The Bella Epoque in the Paris Herald"; David Duff, "Eugenie and Napoleon III", "Queen Mary", "Victoria Travels"; Duc de Castries, "The Lives of the Kings and Queens of France"; Donald Edgar, "The Queen's Children"; Elizabeth Edwards and Margaret Brown, "Tails of the Famous"; Carolly Erickson, "Great Harry"; "Life Book of the Royal Families"; Diana Thomas Warner, "The British Navy", "The Royal Baby Album"; The Times; Christopher Warwick, "King George VI and Queen Elizabeth", "Two Centuries of Royal Weddings"; Audrey Whiting, "The Kents. A Royal Family"; E.N. Williams, "The Penguin Dictionary of English and European History. 1485–1789"; Neville Williams, "The Life and Times of Elizabeth I"; Philip Ziegler, "King William IV".

OTHER BOOKS BY
BARBARA CARTLAND

Romantic Novels, over 400, the most recently published being:

Autobiographical and Biographical:

Historical:

Sociology:

You in the Home
The Fascinating Forties
Marriage for Moderns
Be Vivid, Be Vital
Love, Life and Sex
Vitamins for Vitality
Husbands and Wives
Men are Wonderful
Keep Young and Beautiful by Barbara Cartland and Elinor Glyn
Etiquette for Love and Romance
Barbara Cartland's Book of Health

Etiquette
The Many Facets of Love
Sex and the Teenager
The Book of Charm
Living Together
The Youth Secret
The Magic of Honey
The Book of Beauty and Health

General:

Barbara Cartland's Book of Useless Information with a Foreword by the
Earl Mountbatten of Burma. (In aid of the United World Colleges)
Love and Lovers
The Light of Love
Barbara Cartland's Scrapbook (In aid of the Royal Photographic Museum)
Romantic Royal Marriages
Barbara Cartland's Book of Celebrities
Getting Older, Growing Younger

Verse:

Lines on Life and Love

Music:

An Album of Love Songs sung with the Royal Philharmonic Orchestra.

Films:

The Flame is Love
A Hazard of Hearts

Cartoons:
Barbara Cartland Romances has recently been published in the U.S.A.,
Great Britain, and other parts of the world.

Children:
A Children's Pop-Up Book: Princess to the Rescue

Cookery:

Barbara Cartland's Health Food Cookery Book
　　　　　　　　Food for Love
　　　　　　　　Magic of Honey Cookbook
　　　　　　　　Recipes for Lovers
　　　　　　　　The Romance of Food

Editor of:

The Common Problem by Ronald Cartland (with a preface by the
Rt. Hon. the Earl of Selborne, P.C.)

Barbara Cartland's Library of Love
　　　　　　　　Library of Ancient Wisdom

Written with Love Passionate love letters selected by Barbara Cartland

Drama:

Blood Money
French Dressing

Philosophy:

Touch the Stars

Radio Operetta:

The Rose and the Violet (Music by Mark Lubbock) Performed in 1942.

Radio Plays:

The Caged Bird: An episode in the life of Elizabeth Empress of Austria.
Performed in 1957.